DARK KNIGHTS & SUMMER DAZE

A.J. DAVIDSON

D1607694

Dark Knights & Summer Daze

Copyright © 2017 by A.J. Davidson

Published by Mz. Lady P Presents

This book is dedicated to my boys Jarrett and Ashton. Mommy is trying so hard to make you two proud of her. Everything I do is to show you guys that you can do anything you put your mind to. Never let anyone tell you what you cannot do. That is one thing you will never hear mommy say. Regardless of where you go in life, just know I am always in your corner rooting for you and pushing you to beat the odds. I love you both with every fiber in my bones, even though they are aching right now as I type this. Lol, I love you, babies. Muahhhh
xoxo -Mommy

I prayed on a fallen star
That you never have a broken heart
Though the world is cold, just remember who you are
And I pray that you never have a rainy day
And no matter what the people say
Even when it hurts, it'll be okay
And I pray that you never have a rainy day
And no matter what the people say
In your darkest hours, I'll help guide your way,
this what a mother prays.
K. Michelle – A Mother's Prayer

ACKNOWLEDGMENTS

Yasss! BOOK 11

This is still really hard to believe. Little ole country/proper Ashley from Columbus, MS is an author now. First, I would like to thank God because without this gifted mind that he gave me I would not be able to hear my characters. Lol! That is a gift and a curse at the same time. Especially, when they start talking to you in your sleep, and you have to get up and write that part down or make a mental note to do it first thing in the morning.

Secondly, to my family who has been a very big support system for me. My husband for putting up with me and my typing nonstop all day long or talking about characters that he knows nothing about. But, he still sat there and listened to the story. My sisters Alicia and Asia— that Asia will make sure she gets my book as soon as it comes out, and I love her so much for that. My baby brother Kayin, I love you, baby boy.

Mama, I thank you for always saying I CAN DO IT. You wanted to purchase a book just so that you could take it to work and brag on your daughter. Lol, I gotta make sure I get you that book.

Daddy, I'm doing all I can to make you proud of me. I also have a mental note in my head from you, "NO FREE BOOKS". He says I worked too hard to give books away for free. Know your worth baby girl, and I promise you it's not free.

My last book was dedicated to my grandmothers. My great grandmother passed away a few weeks after my second book was released. Before I left her house, she said how proud of me she was, and she wished me luck with my books. And for that, I will keep on pushing for you Mama Ida, Rest In Heaven I LOVE YOU! Even on the days, when I feel like giving up, I will keep going making sure I never let you down.

TO MY READERS

I cannot thank you guys enough. Whether you shared a post, purchased a paperback, or eBooks, I want to say thank you, thank you a million times. Without you guys, I would not be able to drop these books consistently. Once you finish a book, you come right to my wall or inbox and ask WHEN IS THE NEXT ONE COMING, and that alone pushes me to keep going. I promise to keep putting out amazing work for you guys.

Thank you!

Bookies

I would like to thank you guys for all that you do. Not for just me but for all authors. You guys really go hard for us, and it does not go unnoticed. Zatasha a.k.a ZEE BAE, you are truly one of a kind. I don't know how you have the time to read so many books, but you do. You never turn anyone down and will give any book a chance. I don't care if the title says *My Baby Mama A Crackhead: But I Still Love Her*, you will still read it! Lol! I appreciate you so much! I see Bookies growing and going so far!

TO MY DOPE PEN SISTERS

Latoya Nicole, you are the Yin to my Yang the crucial to my conflict lol! I swear I don't know what I would do without you. When I see you, I see an amazing mother, friend, sister and now **COUSIN**!!! To always know that you are only a call away makes me happy as hell. I love hearing Miracle say I love you Ashley, or Ashley don't like Mr. Bean lol! I love her lil butt so much. Knowing your story and how far you've come to get where you are now, truly amaze me. Keep pushing and dropping those bangers. I love you **COUSIN**

Panda Panda Panda, regardless of what you will always and forever be my sister-in-law, lol. Thank you for always listening and helping me whenever I need it. I think you are an amazing, author and I can't wait to watch your stories come to life on a big screen. I love you Panda.

I can't forget about **Shaye B.** Gurl yo lil butt act just like a real little sister lol, but I'm glad we connected. You are super dope, and your writing style is amazing. Keep up the good work, sis. Y'all don't sleep on my little she sister has raw talent.

If you haven't read any of their books, you better get them because you are truly missing out on a good read.

Oh, trust me I can't forget about my entire **MLPP** team. Let's keep grinding and pushing out these dope books. We are under the hottest publisher out, so there's no excuse for us to fail when she is giving us all the tools we need to succeed.

MY SUPER AWESOME BAD AZZ PUBLISHER

I can't forget the DOPEST publisher of them all, **MZLADYP**!!! I love the fact that she can go into teacher mode real quick and teach you what you need to know to make yourself better as an author to make your brand stand out and to make your books bomb. She wants you to succeed, so she makes sure she gives you the real. I swear I love her for that. Keep up the great work! You are amazing! Thanks for taking me under your wing!!

POEM

Who would've known, that you had to go so suddenly, so fast
   How could it be, that sweet memories would be all, all that we have left
   Now that you're gone, every day I go on (I go on)
   But life it's not the same (life's just not the same)
   I'm so empty inside, and my tears I can't hide, but I'll try to face the pain
   Though I'm missing you
   (Although I'm missing you)
   I'll find a way to get through
   (I'll find a way to get through)
   Living without you
   Cause you were my sister, my strength, and my pride
   Only God may know why, still I will get by.

1

SUMMER DAZE

The worst thing I thought I would ever have to do one day is bury my mother and father. I never even imagined having to bury my twin sister Sunny. We were supposed to be by each other side for the rest of our lives. We did everything together. When I moved, she literally moved with me. That's why I'm sitting here kicking my own ass for not going out with her that night. Maybe that would have prevented my parents from sitting here crying their eyes out at her funeral. Life sometimes gives you the unexpected. We never think about what could happen because we are so focused on what's happening right now.

I'm 23-year-old Summer Daze from Bellwood, IL. Until last week, it was four of us with my identical twin sister and me being the babies of the bunch. Marquise is the oldest, he's 28, then it's Markell who's 26. Our parents always instilled in us to have each other backs and always stick together. Just recently Sunny started living instead of listening. She started leaving the house late and coming home early in the morning with duffle bags full of money. I had my suspicions of her either stripping or selling a whole lot of ass on *Backpage*. I never questioned her. I knew she would eventually tell me what she was doing.

I've always been overprotective of her, so I don't know what the hell was stopping me this time from being all up in her business.

Sunny was on this *I'm grown, and you're not my mother bullshit,* so I fell back some but not completely. After getting the call telling us that she was found behind a dumpster, raped with her throat cut, that's when my life change for the worst. That was the worst news of my life, and all I could do was cry out to my sister asking her why she didn't just talk to me and let me protect her.

My sister was diagnosed with schizophrenia and her having anxiety on top of that didn't make shit any better for her. She always felt someone was after her. We tried hard to protect her from the world, and regardless of what she was going through, we always treated her like she was a normal person. To us, she was just Sunny Daze. We didn't look at her differently regardless of what was going on with her. But for some reason, Sunny liked to call herself Rainy Daze, thinking she was only here to wreck our lives and bring a downpour of hurt on us. She would have her good days, but when the bad days come, they would come full force.

I hated my sister had to go through that, and I hated it even more that she refused our help. Sometimes, she would feel like she was a burden on us and say things like, she wished she was never born. Nothing we could do or say would make her believe that we are here to help, not harm her.

That night she got killed, I was in the living room studying. She started calling me back to back, and all she was saying is, *the man in the dark, the man in the dark.* She wasn't making any sense at all, so I knew then she was having one of her episodes again. I asked her over and over to tell me where she was so that I would come get her right now.

The phone hung up, and I blew her phone up until she answered again. When she picked up, she was calm and started asking me things like, *Summer, what's my favorite color?* My reply was, *Bitch, it's about to be black if you don't tell me what the fuck is going on.* She hung up on me, and I was sitting here racking my brain on where she could be. There was no noise in the background. It was just her breathing heavy during the first call, and on the second call she was back to normal within minutes. Sunny called back after ten minutes and told me that she was fine and was headed home. I started reading over my notes for my test, doing anything I could to be awake by the time she came home.

Unfortunately for me, no matter how long I would have stayed up that night, she was never going to come home.

"Sorry for your loss," I heard someone say to my father, pulling me out of my thoughts.

"Thank you," he replied.

I just sat there watching as everybody came around to view her body. Some touched her face, while others kissed her forehead. Doing my best to hold it together, I just started rocking back and forth with my arms wrapped around myself. I was completely lost in thought as I stared at her purple casket with her picture painted on the side of it. Our oldest brother Marquise is an artist, and he personalized her entire casket. I know that was hard for him to do, but he wanted to make sure he sent her away nicely. The preacher started doing his sermon while the ushers came and closed the casket. That's when it really hit me that I would never see my sister again.

Jumping up out of my seat, I rushed over to them screaming with tears pouring down my face.

"OPEN THE CASKET. OPEN THE CASKET NOW. SUNNY, GET UP. PLEASE DON'T LEAVE ME LIKE THIS. I'M SORRY THAT I COULDN'T PROTECT YOU. JUST COME BACK, AND I PROMISE I CAN FIX THIS. PLEASE JUST COME BACK!"

I could hear the people gasping for air as I made a total fool of myself. My mother Stacy started crying even harder, and my father Marcus was trying hard to keep her from hyperventilating.

Feeling my body being lifted off my sister's casket just as I managed to get it open. I was thrown over my brother Marquise's shoulder like I was a knock off Gucci bag, as he marched out of the church with me. I kept kicking and screaming until I noticed our other brother Markell right on his heels switching hard than a little girl playing in her mama heels. Scrunching my face up because that kinda threw me off.

"Sis you gotta calm the fuck down G, for real. You are getting ma all upset and she's already taking this shit hard as fuck!" Marquise yelled as he paced back and forth in the kitchen of the church.

"You can't tell me how to feel about my damn sister dying."

"Fuck, Summer!" he blurted out. Rubbing his hand over his face, he paused and sat down next to me. "She was our sister too. You didn't just lose her. I know it may be harder for you because she was your twin. Y'all did everything together, we get that, but you gotta keep it together."

"They didn't have to kill her, Quise. They could have just brung her home," I sobbed, throwing my face into his chest.

"I know, sis. We gone get through this together and I'ma find out who did this shit." Markell pulled me off Marquise and pulled me into his chest. All I smelled was *Michael Kors- Very Hollywood*, perfume on his suit. I know because that's my favorite fragrance. Now I was really starting to worry about his ass. I think this nigga is a whole Peter Pan. Fuck a fairy, the way he smells, this nigga gotta have tights on under his suit.

"We gone be ok, sis. Let's get back out here and send our sister home." Markell pulled me from his chest and grabbed my hand. "You ready?"

Nodding my head, I followed him and Quise back out the kitchen. As much as I dreaded going back in here and leaving without my sister, I knew this is what I needed to do to get closure.

MARQUISE DAZE

My family and I grew up on the west side of Chicago until my folks moved our ass out of the city. My life has been good for a while now. I became a silent partner at this strip club my guy just built called B-Live. Money was flowing in like blood flowing out of a bitch on her period— HEAVY. I felt like I was on top of the world.

That was until my sister got killed. Being the oldest brother, I was supposed to be the strong one in the family. The truth is, I'm breaking down, and I don't even know how to hold it together my damn self. Talking to my sister about pulling it together knowing damn well I wanted to jump in the casket with her. That was my little sister, my baby girl, my little sunshine. If anyone supposed to protect her, it was me. I was too busy fucking off with some bitches instead of making sure my sister was good.

Summer called me that night and told me what was going on. I blew it off because I know how Sunny can get. She cries wolf all the time, and there's never anyone there. I know I shouldn't have been so insensitive to her disorder, and that was my fuck up.

Standing up, I watched as my cousins and their best friends Destiny and Desire' stood up to carry her flowers out of the church. My brother and I, along with our cousins, got up and carried her body out. The shit was hard as hell, but I knew I had to do it. As I carried her out, I stared at the beautiful picture I painted of her on her casket. That's one thing about Sunny, even though she was going through hell mentally, you still would always see her smiling.

We went to the burial site, laid her to rest, and went back to my mother's house for the repast. I wasn't up for people being all in my face with the fake ass, *I'm here for you, if you need me,* bullshit. So, I said my goodbyes to my people, and I dipped. Right now, all I wanted to do was smoke a fat ass blunt and lay up with my bitch. Before you start judging, people grieve in their own way. This is my way of doing it. I'ma fuck the shit out of my bitch until the pain of losing my sister goes away. Especially, when I feel like this shit is partially my fault. That's another demon I must deal with later down the line, but right now, I'm not ready to face him yet.

Pulling up to my condo on Division and N. Dearborn Street, I got out and headed right up the stairs. My girl Tameka didn't come to the funeral because my family doesn't fuck with her like that. Granted, the bitch is a stripper— well ex-stripper, but who are we to judge her for her past. Shorty had to make money somehow and before a nigga like me came into her life. She was down bad, but her face was pretty, so I fucked with her the long way anyway. I overlooked the mattress on the floor and sheets covering the windows. Her pussy was good, and that mattress was top notch if I must say so myself.

I saw something in shorty though and it damn sholl wasn't just my dick. She had potential to be the stepmother of my bad ass little boy Marquise Jr. His mother got a hold of some bad drugs, and that mother fucker is a straight hype now. I got custody of Marquise and wiped my hands with her begging ass. Shorty actually tried to put me on child support for a damn baby she ain't even have. First off bitch, where they gone send your money to? I'm sure shorty ain't got no lease for the crack house she's living in.

"How was the funeral, daddy?" Tameka asked as soon as I came up the stairs.

She was coming out of the bedroom with absolutely nothing on. I wanted to sit here and cry a little bit you know, mourn my little sister then I was going to light into Meka's ass later.

"It was a funeral Meka, what do you expect? Summer took it the hardest, and I did everything I could to keep it together for my family."

"Quise, you know it's ok to let that shit out right. You can't keep bottling up your feelings inside and beat yourself up when things go wrong. Just like the night she got murdered."

"LOOK!" I shouted, interrupting her and causing her to jump and her perfect perky breasts to bounce. "I TOLD YOU NOT TO BRING THAT SHIT UP AGAIN, DIDN'T I. I KNOW WHAT I SAW, AND I DID WHAT I COULD?"

"I'm sorry, Quise. I didn't mean to upset you."

She slowly walked over to me, and just like the good girl that she is, she dropped down to her knees and made daddy feel better.

❧ 2 ❧

SUMMER

I spent two weeks with my mom and dad after the funeral. I tried my best not to go into our old room because I knew that was only going to bring the waterworks down again.

My family tried hard to get me to move in with them but after being here for this long, I was ready to go. Mama was talking my ears off and every Saturday she wanted me to take her to some garage sales. They were thinking that it would bother me to go back home and see all of Sunny's things there. I refused and took my crazy ass home anyway. Now, I'm sitting here in her room crying my fucking eyes out, wondering how the fuck did she get mixed up in some shit that would get her killed.

I pulled myself together and started looking around her room, finding more money than clues the more I looked around. I noticed it was a loose floorboard by her bed, so I pulled it up. Pulling out stacks of money at a time and a card from this new club that just opened.

I don't know what the fuck was going on, but I was about to find out. I called up my girls Desire' and Destiny so that they could ride with me downtown. We all have been friends for a long time and grew up more like sisters than best friends. Des and Destiny are 21 and 23 years old. I know when you heard their names you automatically assumed they were twins. They are so close in age and look alike they could really pass for twins. Everyone loved the Macintosh girls when we were coming up— mostly because they were fucking way before Sunny and I had even thought about opening our legs up for anyone. They only lived a few blocks away, so they were letting themselves into my place in no time.

"What's your plan?" Destiny asked as we got inside of my car.

"I don't have one. I figured I was just going to go in and start asking questions and see what I come up with."

"That shit is not going to work, sis. It's a strip club. You walk in on some cop shit, and they gone boot yo ass out quick as fuck."

"Well, what else am I supposed to do? I just want to know what happened to my sister, someone has to know something."

"You said you found a lot of money and that she left late and came home early in the morning, right? That only means one damn thing," Desire' announced.

"What's does that mean?" I asked with my face scrunched up. I know she wasn't implying what I thought she was. Yea, I thought she was on some wild shit, but I didn't really want to believe that shit. Hell, I was really hoping she just had a job at Applebee's, and people paid her bomb ass tips.

"Uggggh Summer, you can't be that damn dense. She was a hoe," she nonchalantly stated while shrugging her shoulders.

Stopping in the middle of the street, I swerved into a parking spot and got out the car. Coming around on the side Des was on, I opened the door and started firing into her ass. I tried to beat her ass like her dusty ass mother should. Desire' always got some foul shit to say about someone else's life. She's been so damn judgmental since we were kids, and I had just about enough of it, especially when the bitch talking slick about my sister.

I don't give a fuck what she did in her free time, but a bitch better not disrespect her in my presence or I'm beating ass, off top. The more I lit into her, the better I started to feel. I was thinking about my sister the whole time, and all of the anger I was feeling for not being there for her was coming out. I was so hurt and angry that tears were just flowing from my eyes.

"DON'T YOU EVER CALL MY SISTER A HOE IN YOUR FUCKING LIFE!" I yelled as I kept throwing blows to her face.

She was covering her face up with her hands, but I didn't give a shit. I wanted this bitch to feel my pain right now since she wanted to be so fucking insensitive. I didn't give her a chance to get to her feet before I kicked her ass back down on the ground. Destiny finally jumped out the car and broke it up.

"I told you about that mouth of yours, sis. You can't just call this girl's sister a hoe and expect her not to beat that ass. Granted you are my sister, but you were wrong, and you needed that lil ass whooping. Now get up." She reached for her hand and helped her off the ground.

I waited on them both to get back inside the car before I started back driving, heading straight to the club. She lucky I didn't leave her black ass right here cus trust me, I was tempted too.

DESIRE' MACINTOSH

What I don't get is how a mother fucker can get mad over facts. Maybe it did come out wrong, but either she was selling that pussy at top dollar price, or she was a stripper, simple as that. Sunny and Summer have been our best friends since middle school. I would never say something to intentionally hurt her. Knowing she just buried her sister, I should have been more sensitive though. I've always had a problem with saying the first thing that came out of my mouth without thinking.

Sunny and Summer were more like Siamese twins. At 23 years old, their grown asses still dressed alike. So, I really do get why she's so hurt behind this shit. Summer is taking it hard, and I know she is grieving— that's the only thing that stopped me from knocking her ass out when she practically beat my ass.

I know if something happened to Destiny, I would be ready to square the fuck up with everybody too, so again I get it.

We pulled up to B-live, and the club was thick as hell. Judging from the people that were walking in, we were way underdressed, so we just stayed outside and peeped things out before saying we will come back on tomorrow. The way my face is fucked up, I didn't want to take my ass inside anyway. That bitch tried to beat me like I stole her man or some shit. She must have thought she was in Monica and Brandy's video, beating me while singing "The Boy Is Mine" in her head. I laughed to myself in the backseat as we continued to peep out shit for a few more minutes.

I could look at Summer and tell she didn't want to leave but watching these thirsty niggas and half-naked bitches go in and out the club wasn't getting us anywhere. We left and went back to our place instead of hers. She didn't want to admit it, but it was hard as hell for her to stay in that damn apartment.

We swung by the liquor store first so that we could make some margaritas and take our minds off Sunny. Stepping out of the car, I went inside and ran into my homeboy from around the way. I was happy as hell I had put that makeup on my face before I got out the car.

"Damn Des, I ain't seen you in a minute," Knight said as he reached in for a hug.

Knight is sexy as hell. He stood about 6'4, dark skin, low cut wavy hair, skin as smooth as my freshly waxed pussy. It looked like the nigga never had a pimple in his life. He was older than us and mostly hung around our older brother. It's been years since I saw his ass because he was in prison on some drug charges.

"Yea, it's good to see you too. I'm glad your home," I replied, looking at him from head to toe. "You still look good, I see."

"You damn right. You know ain't shit to do in jail but workout and read. That's all a nigga been doing. I'm good now though. I got my hands in a few things trying to make a name for myself and shit."

By this time Summer and Destiny walked inside the store. Knight turned his head around to look at them, and when his eyes landed on Summer, they lit up like a Christmas tree.

"Who is that?" He nodded towards Summer.

"You remember Summer Daze from out west, Marquise and Markell's little sister."

"Ooh yea, I haven't seen Summer in a minute though. Wasn't it two of them little mother fuckers?" I rolled my eyes at the way he said it.

"Yea it WAS two of them, Sunny was the other one."

"Damn what happened to shorty?" He questioned.

"Another day," was all I said, letting him know right now was not the time to talk about it.

We walked up to the counter together, and he paid for our liquor they put on the counter. He kept stealing glances at Summer, and I already knew it was only a matter of time before he magically bumped into her again.

Before we could get out the door all the way, she was the one asking who he was. Summer wasn't out as much as my sister and I were, so she didn't know Knight like that. Before he went to jail, that nigga was the hottest nigga walking the streets. He stayed fresh and smelling good as hell. Everybody was dying to be on the tip of his dick, but Knight wasn't that type of nigga. If he had a girl, he was loyal as fuck to her, and it wasn't nothing no one could do or say to get him to fuck with them. Trust me, I tried! Since I couldn't get him, I settled for his younger brother. He's sexy as hell too.

"Either that nigga is sexy as hell, or my ass been dick deprived far too long, and anything looks good to me now," Summer stated as we got back inside of her car.

"Nah, Knight has always been sexy as fuck. He was checking yo lil thick ass out too though. I'm surprised he didn't ask for your number."

"I can't talk to his ass anyway. I just lost my sister. I have to focus on finding out what happened to her."

"You don't think that's the police job?"

"NO!" she snapped quickly. "They will toss this case out in a minute. If I don't find out what happened at least I know I tried."

We pulled up to our place and went inside. Destiny started making the drinks as Summer, and I went into the living room. We started playing music from the Pandora app on the TV to switch up the vibe in here.

"I'm sorry about earlier," Summer turned to me and said.

"No boo, I'm sorry! I was dead wrong." She scrunched her face up quick. "Oh shit, sorry. Wrong choice of words. I was wrong for what I said. I don't know what Sunny was doing, and I was wrong for assuming. I really hope you get closure. I can see you now getting so wrapped up in finding out what happened that you lose focus on school. You're one step away from graduating with your Bachelors, and you don't want to backtrack."

"You're right. Just give me a week to see what I can find out, and if I can't get any information, then I'll let my sister rest and carry on with my life. It's going to be hard as hell because Sunny was my G. I'm going to miss her dancing around the living room, singing to the top of her lungs. She was always a ball of joy until that damn anxiety kicked in. She would go from 0-100 really quick." We both laughed.

"One minute she's dancing, and the next she's hiding in the damn closet, saying someone is outside watching her through the window. It was tough seeing her like that, and it was tougher for me to be strong and not get frustrated with her."

Destiny came in and passed us our glasses of frozen Strawberry Margarita. We sat back reminiscing on the good times we had with Sunny. Although I didn't have many good memories of her, I was definitely here for the drinks, and I got drunk as fuck too. Let me explain that part. See even though we all grew up together, I slowly stopped fucking with Sunny after I heard some things about her. To be honest, I ain't trust the bitch. Sick in the head or not, she still should know right from wrong and what she did was wrong.

After having four glasses, I was ready for someone to murder this pussy. Fuck, bad choice of words again. Good thing I didn't say that shit aloud.

I would call Domano ass but ain't no telling where his ass is. So, I'll settle for my trusty dildo and make the best of this night one cum after another.

3

SUMMER

Yesterday seemed like a big ass blur to me. I got drunk as fuck with Desire' and Destiny, and I thought that would help ease the pain. The only thing that shit did though was make a bitch horny and cry. I was so fucked up that I didn't know if I was crying because I didn't have anyone to call for some drop off dick, or because of my sister. Now, don't think I'm single because I can't get a man or anything like that. I've been trying my best to focus on this last year of school, and I didn't want any dicktractions.

The last guy I dated was a fucking mess. He had no goals in life, and all he wanted to do was be a dope boy, and that wasn't gone work for me. I had to let that mother fucker go with the quickness. After him, I was focused on getting out of college and moving far away from this state.

"Hey sweetie, how are you feeling?" my mom asked as she walked into the kitchen where I was sitting.

"Hey, ma. I'm good. I've been trying to prepare myself to clean out Sunny's room. I don't want to throw her clothes away, so I figured I would just donate them. I know I can't keep it in the apartment, or I would literally run myself crazy. How's dad holding up?" I asked as I took the tea she was handing me.

"You know your father. He just threw himself into work so that he wouldn't have to deal with his emotions."

"Don't I know it. I just came by to drop off some of this money. I'm sure you can use it for something."

"Where did you get this from Summer? I know yo ass ain't into that front-page stuff."

"First off, it's Backpage and hell no. Apparently, Sunny was into something though, ma. I found all of that in her room."

"Noo! Don't lie on your sister like that. She was barely capable of running the register at Target, so I know damn well she wasn't throwing that ass in an oval."

"Ma, please stop! It's throw that ass in a circle, and it couldn't have been too hard because she had more than this stashed away."

"Well, where is the rest?"

"Umm, I have it. Did you think I was giving it all to you? Be happy you got that. I have more debt from school than my eyes can see, so I could have used it all. I was just being nice by giving you some of it."

"Take it, Summer," she stated, passing the bag back to me. "You need it more than I do. We are doing well over here, and your father brings home a decent amount of money, so we are good, baby." I thanked her and waited on her to finish cooking dinner.

Des, Destiny and I have plans to go back to the club tonight to see if anyone knows her and who she left with that night. I just want an ounce of information to take to the police, and I will let them fake like they are handling the rest of this shit.

⚜

"DO I LOOK OK?" I ASKED THEM AS DID A LITTLE SPIN. WE STARTED to get dressed for the club, and I was nervous as hell. Call me lame all you want, but I don't do places like this.

"Yea, it's ok! You look thotish, but if you take those damn coffee colored stockings off you will look like a thot for real. Show some skin, girl!" Desire' teased, as she slipped into her tight backless red dress.

Both of them had banging ass bodies. I don't know if the shit was hereditary or it was because they were fucking since we were fifteen. They filled out quick as hell while my sister and I just waited on God to make our shit sprout out on its on.

"Well, my mom always said to wear stockings when you wear a dress."

"You wanna put a slip on too so we can drop yo ass off at a revival on our way to the club?" Destiny joked. "Summer, you are going to a strip club boo, not Sunday school. You gotta get with the program sis. You're 23 years old and already on a strike from dick. This is your glory years. You're supposed to be throwing that pussy to everybody and slow down once you hit 25. You got two more good pussy years in you, and after that, your pussy is no good. Haven't you heard if you don't use it you lose it?"

"Yea, but I'm almost positive that wasn't about pussy."

"I don't know if it was or not, but I'm sure after you hit a certain age your pussy juices dry up like overcooked chicken." Shrugging my shoulders, I started taking my stockings off so that they would shut the hell up.

"BITCH! IS THAT A BUSH?" they both yelled out.

"You know what, fuck y'all! Yea, it's a bush. Hell, I ain't fucking, so there's no need to get that shit waxed. Keep your eyes on your own loose pussies and stop worrying about my shit. I can go do this shit on my own and not worry about either one of you thotties worrying me."

I brushed past them and grabbed my purse. I was not about to sit and go back and forth about the shit I put on my body or the amount of coochie hair I have.

"Come on here bush-wick. We were just joking with you. It's your pussy; just make sure you get buckwheat out that head lock before you give that pussy away again."

Tossing my throw pillow at Des, I couldn't do anything but laugh at her dumb ass as we walked out of the door.

Pulling up at the club, I paid the valet then waited in line to get in. The line was long as hell, and the bouncer kept coming and selecting the people that he wanted to let in. His eyes landed on me, and he stopped quickly.

"Sunny, fuck yo crazy ass standing in the line for. Get inside so you can get ready to go on stage." I almost cursed his ass out until I realized what the fuck he was talking about. Des and Destiny nudged me to go inside with him.

"Can I bring my girls in too?"

"You already know boss man let yo ass do whatever you wanna do. Y'all come on." We grabbed each other's hand and walked inside behind him. As soon as I walked in the door, I was pulled to the side by a big stocky dude.

"Where yo ass been, Sunshine? I have been worried as fuck about you. These customers have been requesting you, and you were nowhere to be found."

Not knowing what to say I just nodded my head and said. "Umm. I'm sorry... I guess."

He started shaking his head before pulling me to the back room where other girls were half naked and changing into a shoestring before walking out the door. I was completely disgusted at how they paraded around showing everything without a care in the world. This damn room look like it was filled with diseases and loose coochies.

"Get dressed. I'm letting them know you are here. Hurry up, because you've been missing in action long enough. I'm making yo ass go out on the stage next."

My neck snapped around quickly, and I damn near shitted a brick. Here I am with a coochie full of hair and he is talking about I'm about to go on stage next. He's got life all the way fucked up. The other girls started leaving out the dressing room one by one. After a while, Desire' and Destiny snuck back here with me trying to see what the hell was going on.

"Bitch, this mother fucker is trying to get me to go on stage next."

"Girl, see this is why I told you to get rid of that bush. You never know when you gone be bussing that pussy open. Luckily my ass is a freak, and I always keep a fresh razor in my purse just in case I got some little hairs coming back, and I hook up with a dude. I excuse myself to the bathroom, wet my pussy, put a little soap on there and shave that shit off. Have her smoother than a baby's bottom in no time. Remember, only hair that should touch a man lips is his mustache. Now go handle that," she stated, pulling the razor out of her purse making me go into the bathroom.

I see why Diamond was scared to dance when she first started working at *The Players Club*. This shit is not for the average person for real.

TRENCH KNIGHT

I walked into the club with intentions on picking up my money and dipping. Ever since I got out of prison, I've been trying to keep my distance from a lot of shit, especially since more shit goes on at these damn strip clubs than bitches swinging on poles for a couple of hundred dollars. I ain't about to risk my freedom for no mother fucker. When I got out, I threw some money to my guy Skillz to help build this club. I'm a behind the scenes type, and as long as the money was flowing in, I was good to go.

"What's good, boss?" Skillz said as I stepped into the VIP room where he was sitting.

"Not shit, just swinging through to get this bread. I see you got some new bitches up in here." I stated once I saw this girl step out on the stage. She looked like she was terrified, and the thirsty ass men weren't making it any better.

"Nah, she ain't new, that's Sunny's ass. She's been MIA for a minute, but OG caught her ass standing outside in the line like she didn't even work in this mother fucker."

I watched as she eased her way on stage more as the DJ started playing "Take It Off" by 8Ball and MJG. She started moving slowly, and I damn near wanted to laugh shorty couldn't dance a lick.

"You sure shorty ain't new. She's out there dancing like a newborn calf trying to walk," I joked.

"Yea, I don't know what she on. She usually be up there flipping and showing everything but the inside of her asshole."

I started laughing at his ass until it hit me. She looked just like the shorty I saw at the liquor store last night. When I saw Desire' in the store she said Summer had a sister meaning that mother fucker is long gone. Either she done resurrected herself from the dead, or that's Summer ass on the stage.

"GET YO ASS OFF THE STAGE!" a drunk dude yelled at her, making the rest of the men do the same. The bouncer came around and made his drunk ass leave.

Summer kept trying her best to be sexy, but that shit wasn't working. The next thing I know a mother fucker threw a whole tomato at her head. She stopped dancing like she was in shock until another one hit her ass, then she instantly ran off the stage.

"Aye G, I'ma catch up with you in a minute." I dapped him up and headed out of his area.

I went straight to the back room where she would be. It was more girls in there laughing at her as she stood in the mirror trying to pull the busted tomato out of her hair. I watched her from behind as I approached her. Shorty had a banging ass body for real. My dark skin ass got a thing for red bones and she bright as hell. Without the 6in stripper heels, I give her a good 5'5. Nice little slim thick frame and surprisingly, all that hair look like it just might be hers.

My cousin do hair and I've seen plenty of bitches come in but they lace fronts stayed outside. Her shit don't look like that at all.

"Y'all clear this bitch out and let me talk to her for a second." One girl popped her lips until I looked at her with stern eyes. "Bitch, if you don't get the fuck out of here yo lil musty pussy ass won't have a fucking job." She and everyone else skipped their asses out of here quick.

"You good, ma?" I asked as I watched the tears pour down her face through the mirror.

"A tomato... like G, who the fuck just walks around with fucking

TOMATOES?" she yelled as she kept pulling more chunks out of her hair.

I tried not to laugh cus that shit was funny as hell. She had so many chunks of tomato in her hair that she could make Rotel dip.

"All I came here to do is find out what the hell happened to my sister, and I ended up on stage half naked with cuts from that damn razor on my pussy. I was trying to dance sexy all the while my fucking pussy was burning from the damn itchy ass outfit scraping my cuts. On top of that, I was putting in some good work out there if I must say so myself, and they didn't throw shit but a tomato at my ass."

"You did aight," I joked. "I'm not even gone ask about the cuts on your pussy. Although I can make them feel better." I winked.

As long as they were cuts from a razor and her ass wasn't out here burning when she pissed and shit, we were good. Shaking that thought from my head, I got back to giving her my attention. "What happened to your sister though, if you don't mind me asking?"

"A few weeks ago, they found her in the alley not too far from here. She had her throat cut, and was raped. I didn't know she even worked here until after she got killed. Apparently, no one in this bitch even cared because they didn't even know she was dead. We asked them not to put it on the news to respect her privacy and shit, but it's not like people were going to actually come forward and say anything."

"Damn, ma. I know that has to be tough for you to deal with. I'm not sure if you getting out on that stage tonight helped you any either."

"It was a start."

"Question. How are you supposed to find out what happened to her if you in here pretending to be her? That would have people thinking she is still alive, right?"

"I guess I never thought about that. I really wasn't trying to be her. The big ass bouncer just called me her name when he saw me and let me inside the club. Then another big ass dude pulled me to the back to get dressed and said people have been asking for me...well, Sunny. I could have told him right then that I wasn't her. I guess a part of me wanted to see just what the hell she was caught up in."

"Yea, I get it. I will ask around to see if anyone saw her leave with anyone. I own this too, so I'm sure I can listen out for some shit. I hope you find what you are looking for. Just know some things are left buried for the best. Like the less you know, the less it hurts."

She looked at me, and I could tell she wanted to break down and cry. Shit, honestly, I wanted her to just so I could scoop her little sexy ass up and walk her out of the club. I was more than willing to be her knight in shining armor if it would help me get close to her.

❄ 4 ❄

MARQUISE

I was sitting in the club throwing back shots of liquor while I got a lap dance from this big booty bitch. She was slim in the waist with a fat ass like Diamond off *Love & Hip Hop: Atlanta.* She was giving me her all, and I was slipping hunnids after hunnids in her g string. She was working hard for that shit too. That was until I heard the music switch and they introduced the next dancer.

"Get that money out fellas. She's been out, but she's back and better than ever. Coming to the stage, it's Miss 2 Faaaaaace!"

When I heard that name, I damn near shitted a brick of cocaine, although if I could do that, I would be a rich mother fucker. Nigga would be around here drinking detox tea just to shit a brick to re-up.

My sister's favorite song started playing, and my heart started racing. I thought I was losing my fucking mind. She wouldn't let the DJ play that song for no other dancers, just her like it was her signature song or something. That's what had my ass bugging the fuck out. By this time, I completely tuned shorty out and put my money up. I was so focused on the stage that I lost interest in the bitch before me. The lights were bright as hell, and it looked like she was scared to come out.

"Let me see you take it off, take it off, take it off, take it off. Gone and show me that candy babe, gone and show me that candy."

As 8Ball and MJG's "Take It Off" starts to play, she started dancing around and finally came into my view.

"Sunny?" I said aloud to myself. Shaking my head back and forth, I just knew I was seeing things.

Once she started dancing I was on the floor laughing. I don't know how in the hell Summer ended up here, but I had to get her ass off stage and quick. She never knew how to dance. Sunny would always dance around the house, and Summer would be in the room reading or doing homework.

That's one way I was always able to tell them apart. When they would try to pull a switch-a-roo on us and make us guess which one was the other person, I would always make them start dancing. Sunny would be doing the footwork or whatever new dance was out, and Summer's ass would be over there looking like she was doing the dosey doe.

"GET YO ASS OFF THE STAGE!" I heard a man yell, bringing me back to the situation at hand.

"Aye, yo OG, get him the fuck outta here!" I spat to the bouncer, and he did as he was told.

Stopping the waitress as she was walking past, I whispered in her ear, and she ran off quickly. Turning back to face Summer, I couldn't do shit but shake my head. She was up there wobbling, and that shit was not pretty at all. Before she got ready to take her top off the waitress was returning.

Taking the tomatoes from her, I turned around and acted like I was Ray throwing the ball at Can't Get Right, from the movie Life. I threw a curve ball at her ass so smooth, hitting her right in the head. She was a little dazed at first, so I chunked the other one at her hitting her again. That one made her run off quick as hell. I started to go after her but didn't want to deal with all of the questions about if I knew Sunny was working here.

The truth is, I knew. Hell, I gave her the job. She got tired of us treating her like she was special, and she wanted to get out there and make her own money. I let her do her thing, and I tried my best to keep a close eye on her at all times. When it was time for her to go on stage, I would leave. I made sure she was in good hands before I left and went to the back. OG always kept a close eye on her when I wasn't around.

I gave her the name 2 Face because she was a twin. I thought it was dope. I knew Sunny was into some other shit. She would leave the club with some random ass nigga and go fuck. I tried talking to her ass, but she would just spazz out on me.

The bouncer OG told me about it because he's always at the door watching who came and went. This particular night the dude she left with made sure he kept his face from being seen. I've been watching tape after tape trying to see who she left with, and I'm coming up with nothing. I've been blaming myself ever since I got the phone call. I should have been more of a big brother and protected her instead of watching her do wrong and knowing of her condition. That was my fuck up, and I have to deal with that for the rest of my life.

Summer is very over the top, and if she found out I knew, she would really put this shit on me. A nigga already feels bad, and she will make my ass feel even worse.

SMACK!

I grabbed my face as it stung from getting the shit smacked out of me. Pulling my gun out quickly, I turned to face the bitch who was about to lose her fucking life. I knew it was a bitch cause don't know nigga in the world hit yo ass with a open hand- Unless he trying to be one of those Kaitlyn Jenner bitches. I lowered my gun once I turned around and came face to face with Summer.

Fuck!

SUMMER

After washing my hair with one of those bitches shampoo, I was finally ready to leave this place. Walking out the back with Knight after getting dressed, my eyes scanned the club for Desire' and Destiny, but those hoes were nowhere to be found. Doing one last scan before I left and went home without them, my eyes suddenly landed on my brother Marquise. *What the fuck is he doing here?* I said to myself.

"Can you wait right here for me? I will be right back," I said to Knight as I walked through the little crowd to get to him.

Looking down at the table he was sitting at, I saw two more tomatoes sitting there, not to mention he still had squashed up pieces on his hands from where his dirty ass squeezed it before throwing it at me. I was heated and ready to fight his ass for real.

SMACK!

I hit his ass so hard that the nigga pulled his gun out on me until he looked and saw it was me, then he put it away.

"Yo Summer, chill out with that shit bruh!" he barked. That shit wasn't fazing me though. I probably can't dance, but I got some hands that will rock even the biggest bitch or nigga.

"Why in the hell would you hit me with that shit?"

"Sis, I had to get you off stage. You were looking a mess for real.

You should thank me. I saved you some embarrassment. You know you were never the better dancer out of the two of you." Sunny popped in my head when he said that.

"Fuck you, and we need to talk, so when you finish given these dirty bitches your money, come over to my place first thing in the morning."

"Before I found out it was you on stage, you were almost one of those dirty bitches to get my money."

Rolling my eyes at him, I just turned to walk away. Marquise always run out with the shit he says, and I was not in the fucking mood. I wanted to get home and act like this day never happened.

Walking back up on Knight, I let him know I was ready to go. He asked me to go and have breakfast with him. It's 1 am and I'm usually deep under the covers right now. Seeing that I just worked up an appetite on stage, I think I deserve a big ass breakfast. Laughing at myself, I thought who am I kidding. From the way I was dancing, the only meal my ass deserve is a plain ass biscuit. If he gets me anything else, it's because he feels sorry for my ass.

Waiting on valet to pull my car around, Des and Destiny emerged from the side of the building.

"The fuck you hoes doing over there?" I questioned as they both walked up to me. Desire was stumbling, so I knew that bitch was drunk as hell.

"Desire's drunk ass had to throw up. I hope you are done on stage making a fool of yourself because we are ready to go home," Destiny stated.

"I thought y'all left, so I told Knight I would go to breakfast with him."

"I could take you home, I don't mind," he spoke up and said. I kinda wanted to drive my own shit, but since they are ready to go, and we are going the opposite direction, I guess I could leave with him.

"Don't fuck my shit up, Destiny," I blurted out as the valet pulled up. They got in the car to head home while Knight and I walked over to his truck.

"So, Miss Summer, besides stripping, what do you do for fun?"

"You got jokes I see. This was my first and last time ever doing some shit like this. I'm in school for Elementary Education, so studying is my fun. My ass don't do shit, and that's sad. I'm 23 years old, and I live my life like I'm an old ass lady. If it wasn't for Desire' and Destiny my ass would be in here looking like I'm headed to church with some damn stockings on and shit."

"Damn, you definitely need to get out more. This world is too big not to enjoy life. Shit, it's so much shit to do around Chicago that would bring some type of excitement into your life. You really have no excuse unless yo ass is just that lame that you choose not to smile or laugh about shit."

The more he talked about me enjoying life, the more my eyes roamed around his sexy ass lips as he spoke. I had completely tuned his ass out and started thinking about riding his damn face.

"What do you think about that?" he questioned, pulling me from my thoughts after not hearing a word he said.

"Ugh yea, um that sounds good."

"Ok, cool. After we eat, I will take you home. Just make sure you are packed and ready by noon. It's going to be hot so don't pack jeans and shit like that. You can wear anything but that shit you had on while you were on stage. Throw that shit all the way away."

I laughed, but I really wanted to ask his ass where we were going but didn't want to look crazy because my ass just agreed to some shit that I didn't even hear.

We waited a little while longer on our food as we continued to talk. The more we sat and talked, the more he helped keep my mind off my sister. I don't know if that was a good or bad thing, but for the first time in weeks, I was actually thinking about myself for once. I've been holding Sunny's hand for years now, or so I thought, trying my best to make sure she was good especially when she would have her episodes.

All I ever wanted to do was protect my sister and finish school. Nothing else mattered to me. Now that she's gone, I actually have a little chance to breathe and live for me and to put Summer first for once. I hope that doesn't sound bad. I'm still going to do all I can to find out what happened, but I will live my life while I'm at it.

"Here you go. If you need anything else just let me know."

"Thank you," Knight replied while reaching for his fork. "I'm actually excited about our trip. I haven't been on vacation in years, so this is much needed. Vegas is going to be nice as hell. We can do a little shopping, gambling, and sightseeing— whatever you want to do. It's all about you while we are there." I was happy as hell he finally said where we were going. A bitch was gone be looking like a fool with all type of crazy shit in the suitcase.

"I've never been so I'm excited as well, but you do know you don't have to do this, right. I'm ok just sitting around here bored."

"Nah ma, you need a break from this shit and so do I. I won't try anything, I promise to keep this big dick in my pants at all times. I'll even get you your own suite, if that would make you more comfortable."

My mind was still stuck on him saying he had a big dick. I was over here flexing my pussy muscles trying to get prepared for him to tear this pussy up. Fuck, what he is talking about. You know what they say, what happens in Vegas stays in Vegas. So, we can fuck up a storm, and no one will have to know a thing. This pussy hasn't been tampered with in a long as time. it's time to break the seal before a bitch turn back into a virgin.

5

MARQUISE

"Hmm!" I moaned out as Meka was using that beautiful mouth of hers to wake me up.

She claims she get a kick out of my dick growing in her mouth. You know when it goes from squishy to hard as a brick. Shiiid, I enjoy that shit too. I love watching her pretty ass inhale my shit like a human ant eater. The more she sucked, the more my shit bricked up. Her mouth was hot, but I needed to be deep in them guts instead. Moving her off me, I got up and jumped right behind her. Slamming my dick inside her, she let out a moan that the neighbors could hear.

"Shit Quise, slow down. That shit hurts."

Using her ponytail like it was straps on a horse. I started digging deeper into her guts, not giving a fuck what she was talking about. My dick is big, so it's gone hurt whether a nigga is going fast or slow.

"Who made these burnt ass pancakes? I mean they nasty but I'ma still eat them cause a bitch is hungry as fuck."

I looked up right as Summer was walking in. She came in and sat down at the head of my bed unbothered by the murder I was committing on this pussy. Rolling her eyes at us, she kept eating, so I kept right on fucking. Tameka was trying her best to cover up and push me off her, but I was getting this nut— fuck Summer. I told her to hold on to my key in case of emergency only anyway. I'm sure the shit she wanted ain't no fucking emergency, especially since she decided to fix her a plate first.

"Marquise, it's almost 10:30, why weren't you at my house like I told you to be? I have plans this afternoon, so I was hoping to get our little talk over."

"G, you really about to sit right here and talk in the middle of all this?" I questioned.

"She ain't enjoying the shit anyway, the way she is looking. I'm sure that pussy done dried up by now. Her pussy is about as dry as these damn pancakes. Shorty can't cook a lick, bruh." She spit the chewed-up pancakes back on the plate and slid the plate towards Tameka. "Here, you can have this shit back. I'll grab me some IHOP on the way home."

"FUCK!" I yelled, starting to get frustrated with her talkative ass. "Yo Meka, get up." I spat. She jumped up grabbing her sleeping shorts and walked into the bathroom, hitting me on her way in. Shrugging it off, I slipped my dick back into my boxers and sat down.

"Fuck you want, sis?"

"I want you to spray some air freshener in this bitch. Y'all got the room smelling like morning breath and hot ass," she blurted out.

Meka came out the bathroom mugging Summer. Summer looked at me and laughed. I already knew why she was laughing because little do Meka know sis got them hands for real. She has always kept to herself, but that bitch is a quiet storm once you get on her bad side. Bitches always try my sister cause she don't say shit, they be regretting that shit after that ass whooping though.

"Anyway, you know why I came over here. Why didn't you tell me about Sunny?"

"Because she was grown as hell, sis. She asked me not to say anything, and I didn't. I let her make her money and enjoy herself. Y'all sheltered the shit out of that girl. She had a condition, but she wasn't physically disabled. I thought what I was doing was helping her."

"No, it killed her. If she weren't out there pretending to be cousin Ebony, then she would still be alive."

"Ebony?" I questioned with my face frowned up. "We ain't got no cousin Ebony."

"Not our cousin, fool. Diamond from *Players Club*, cousin Ebony." I started laughing hard as fuck.

"You got issues for real. That girl was just trying to live, that's it. Yea, she did some extra shit on the side that had nothing to do with me. I couldn't keep my eyes on her at all times. When I found out what happened, I did my own little investigating. No one saw the face of the man she left with. I saw her leave the club, but his face was never shown. He had a fucking black hoodie on with a tiger on the hood part.

Summer, listen. It's not your job to play detective. You need to get back to your life for real. This is coming from your big brother. You gotta chill. Get your head back in those books and get ready to graduate. That's what Sunny would want you to do. Now promise me you will drop this and get back to your life."

"As bad as I don't want to, I will try. This shit has been running me crazy. I've been having these dreams about her every night. She's just smiling and waving at me." Turning my head to her, I watched as she started wiping the tears that were rolling down her face. "I just wish she was still here. That's it! I just want my sister back."

Getting up, I went over and sat beside her on the bed, wrapping my arm around her while she cried.

"When she came to you in your dreams, it's just her way of telling you that she is ok. It's ok to mourn her sis, but you gotta let her go. I'm not saying right now, I'm not saying tomorrow, but you have to let her rest, baby girl." Sucking up her tears, she wiped the last one away that was threatening to escape.

"Marquise."

"Sup, sis?"

"Get your hands off me." Looking confused, I moved my arm back.

"I was just trying to help yo sensitive ass."

"I know, and you were also over there rubbing on a dry clit like you were trying to get a genie to come out that bitch. I bet yo ass was wishing for the bitch's pussy to get wet. That pussy was sounding like you were dragging your nails on a chalkboard when I walked in.

"Her pussy was not that dry."

"The fact that you said *not that dry* lets me further know that it was partially dry. Anyway, I gotta vacation I have to finish getting prepared for."

"Let me find out you finally thinking of yourself first."

"This guy I met wanted to take me away to get my mind off things. I was hesitant at first, but I'm ready to go and enjoy myself for the first time in a while."

"Who's he?"

"I'm not telling you because ya ass likes to do background checks and shit. I'll text you when we make it to Vegas." She got up and threw me the deuces as she left out.

I walked out the room behind her to get my plate from Tameka. She was sitting at the table looking pissed off and shit. Sitting down in front of the plate she made for me, I started eating the pancakes, and I couldn't do shit but laugh to myself because Summer ass was right. These pancakes dry as fuck. I started drowning them in syrup. I damn near wanted to run out the door with my sister to get me some damn IHOP too.

"You don't have to eat them, Marquise. I forgot to add the egg." She was over there looking like her ass was about to cry for real.

"It's cool, shorty. I like them like this." I started eating them anyway, and if it weren't for the glass of orange juice, my ass would've choked to death.

SUMMER

Knight pulled up to my place and swaggered his way up my stairs to help me with my bags. He came inside the house, and his cologne quickly filled the air. He was smelling good as hell and looking like a whole snack.

"Where are you going with your thot outfit on?" I joked. He had on a white V-neck with some gray sweatpants. His dick print made it look like he was Safaree and he had a whole snake in his pants. He looked down at what I was looking at and smirked at me.

"Get ya eyes off my dick before I pull it out and make the hairs stand up on ya pussy."

"I learned my lesson about having hair on my pussy," I mumbled.

"Huh?"

"Oh nothing, here," I replied, passing him my purple luggage. "Let me grab my laptop and then I'm ready to go."

"If you plan on doing some work, you might as well leave it here. We ain't on that this weekend. It's all about laughing, eating good, drinking good and fucking up headboards."

"What?" I questioned like I didn't hear that last part he threw in really quick.

"Oh nothing, let's go before the pilot leave our ass."

We left out the house and headed right to the airport, or so I thought. We pulled up to another landing strip where a private plane was waiting for us. Getting out, we boarded the plane, and I was really impressed, impressed because he pulled this shit off and cause the inside of this shit was dope as hell. The seats were black with gold trimming with Tiger heads stitched into the headrest.

"This is real nice," I stated as I took a seat.

"Thanks. It's good to know people in high places. Bruh, on his grown man shit now, so this is one of the first things he coped once his money started racking up like crazy. He also owns a clothing line and a shoe store. I'm proud of him for real. The way these niggas are moving in the city, him taking the legit route was the right move. I prayed hard that he didn't turn out like his big brother. I fucked up and fucked a lot of people over coming up. I had to learn the hard way, that street life ain't for me. My black ass would work at McDowell's before I sling any drugs again."

I let out a little laugh before speaking. "You mean McDonald's, right?"

"No, I said what I meant, McDowell's. You know where Akeem and Semmi worked in *Coming to America*." I started cracking up laughing.

"You do know that shit is not real, right?" He looked at me like I had just ruined a wet dream.

"Whatever. Call it what you want, but my ass is still trying to be on my legit shit. I get money through the club, and I own a few Boys and Girls clubs in the city. I'm trying my best to give the youth what I didn't have. Ya dig?"

"That's dope. Looking at you, I never would have taken you for the type to do shit like that."

"How do I look?" I didn't know if he wanted me to tell him how I really thought he looked or what. To me, he is sexy as fuck with the lips of a seat that I can't wait to sit on.

"I mean you just don't look like you fool with other people kids."

"Shit, I don't," he blurted out as he threw back a shot of Patrón. "I said I own the buildings. I didn't say I sit in a circle and play Duck Duck Goose with them bad ass, little silver teeth having ass mother fuckers. I rather have them in my building safe with licensed teachers, actually learning some shit rather than on the streets letting the hood raise them like me."

"You didn't turn out so bad though, Knight."

"Shit, I was bad. It took a lot of life lessons to wake my ass up. It was either get on the straight and narrow, or make prison my permanent home, and I wasn't trying to do that shit."

We talked a little more, and I started drinking a lot more than expected. The conversation was getting good, and I was really enjoying myself. He had me taking shots of Patrón, and the private bartender he had on the plane with us started making me all types of mixed drinks. A bitch was wasted for real. He turned some music on, and my non-dancing ass got up and started dancing.

"Let me find out you were on the stage stunting, and yo little ass really do know how to dance."

I didn't say shit. I just started smiling like a drunken fool and grinding on him. When I felt that big ass dick get hard under me, a bitch jumped up like someone put fire to my ass. He thought that shit was funny as hell.

"Summer, it's just a dick."

"Nah. That shit ain't normal, and a bitch ain't had sex in years, but I do know what a regular dick is supposed to feel like. And that shit ain't it," I stated, pointing to his dick.

Waving me off, he got up and walked towards me. I don't know if it was because I was drunk or what, but the way he walked had my pussy thumbing just begging for some action. He placed his hand under my chin to lift my head up and kissed me softly one time and then pulled back to look into my eyes like he was searching them to see if I wanted him to stop or not. I didn't. I wanted this man in the worst way possible. Leaning down, he kissed me again, and I welcomed it. Kissing him back, I wrapped my arms around his neck as he lifted me off the ground. Walking over to a seat, he sat down as we continued to aggressively kiss each other while I straddled him.

Pulling my shirt over my head, he gazed at my 38D breasts before unsnapping my bra with one hand. Laying me down on the seat, I watched as he started undressing. I was happy the bartender was in another area and couldn't see us because this man was letting that dick hang freely. Once I laid eyes on it, I started looking around the plane for a parachute cause a bitch wanted to jump out mid-flight.

It was long, chocolate, and pretty as hell. It was like Jesus said I'ma work extra hard on this part. Sliding my leggings off, he kneeled his tall ass down and put my legs over his shoulders, kissing the inside of my thighs as he made his way to my clit. I was nervous as hell because again, it's been a minute. I was so glad Des gave me that razor last night or he would have hair all up his nose right now. Once his tongue touched my clit, it felt like my whole body went limp. I couldn't do shit but lay there and take all of the pleasure he was issuing out to me.

Grabbing his head, I started grinding on his tongue, letting low moans ease out of my mouth.

"You like that baby?" he asked while continuing to stuff his face. Not being able to speak, I just nodded my head and bit my bottom lip while I gently squeezed my breasts.

"FUCK!" I blurted out as I started to feel myself cum.

"Keep cumin'," he requested right as my juices started flowing out like the levee just broke. He never stopped eating me. It's like he was making sure he got it all out. Giving me a single kiss on the top of my lips, he moved back and rolled the condom down his horse size dick.

"Knight, please don't hurt me. I told you it has been a while so just know that this pussy is tighter than Asian eyes," I joked, making us both laugh.

"I got you, ma. How bout I let you take control? You put in as much as you can handle."

Picking me up, he took a seat on the long seat and pulled me on top of him. Gripping his dick gently, my eyes got big as hell when my hand couldn't go all the way around. I allowed his head to soak in my juices before I started to ease down on him. His head alone had me waiting to cum again. Moving slowly, I worked him inside of me and watched as his eyes started rolling to the back of his head. Once I had all of him inside of me, I sat there for a moment and kissed him as my pussy adjusted to his massive size. As soon as he saw I was ready to go, he started beating my shit up. He had a bitch reaching for the hem of Jesus's robe.

❦ 6 ❦

KNIGHT

We had about thirty more minutes left on the flight once we got finished. She was laying on me with her head cuffed under my neck. I never expected us to fuck, but now that it's over, I never want our ass to stop. Shorty's tight ass pussy got some power, for real.

"We gotta get dressed. We're about to land in a minute." She rose up and kissed me again before standing up to get dressed. She was walking around slowly like she had just lost her virginity or something. "That lil pussy is sore, ain't it?"

"Hell yea, fuck you. You know what you were doing."

Grabbing our bags as we exited the plane, we headed right to a car that was waiting for us. I booked us a SKYLOFT at MGM Grand Hotel. Shorty looked like she ain't been nowhere nice before, so a nigga wanted to impress her ass. We pulled up to the hotel, grabbed our keys, and went right up.

"Damn, this shit is nice for real. Let me find out yo ass had intentions on getting some pussy the entire time. Walking into a room like this, a bitch would feel like she's obligated to open these legs up. If a nigga spends a grip on a room like this, he can fuck me every minute on the hour, for real."

A.J. DAVIDSON

"You silly, let's clean up so that we can enjoy this shit for real. The room is nice, but we got bigger plans outside of the room."

Leaving the hotel, the driver took us to this place where we took a helicopter ride to the Grand Canyon Skywalk. The shit was dope for real. Just seeing her light up with excitement was good enough for me. She's so beautiful, and it's hard for me not to just stare at her ass. I noticed since we left, she hasn't mentioned her sister once. The other day she couldn't go five minutes without mentioning her name. My goal was to ease her mind and help her enjoy the rest of her life.

☙❧

"Thank you for this," she stated as she turned away from the window and looked at me. "Even if we don't do anything else the rest of the trip, I've already enjoyed myself. That skywalk is something I wouldn't have done, ever. It's crazy how in so little time you are bringing me out of my shell and also helping me cope with my sister. I can't lie like I haven't been thinking about her and talking to her in my head, but this really has helped me a lot. So again, thank you."

Kissing me on the cheek, she instantly made my dick jump. The helicopter landed, and we jumped back in the car, and I let her pick what we did next. Her ass wanted to do like most women and shop. We walked around from place to place, and I held her bags like I was her dude.

"Say ma; you don't think you got enough shit?"

"Nah, just one more place and I promise I'm done. This last stop is for you." She found a Victoria Secret, and I waited outside until she was done. About 20 minutes later, she came back out with a bag and a big ass smile plastered across her face.

"We can go back to the hotel now I'm ready to show you your gift." I saw the size of that little ass bag, and it looks like she ain't gone let Victoria keep her secret for long.

☙❧

After spending the last few days with Summer, it was finally

44

time to get back to the money. We did damn near everything you could do in Vegas, including fuck up a headboard. She was cool as hell for real, and I enjoyed myself. I love the fact that she ain't no ghetto ratchet ass female. She was down to earth, more educated than the average bitch, and her pussy was more delicious than sweet potato pie.

"What the hell got yo ass over there grinning like that?" my little brother TK asked as he walked in my office taking a seat.

"My mama told me to tell you to mind yo daaaamn mother fucking business bitch, two plus two not knowing ass bitch."

"Nigga, shut yo stupid ass up. For real though, where you been?"

"Out with my shorty."

"Ahh man, cut that shit out."

"For real, she's on her way here right now to drop me off some Portillo's. She's bad as hell too."

"Let me be the judge of that shit. You know yo bitches be having banging ass bodies, but that face be fucked up."

"Fuck you bruh, how bout that," I joked.

We both looked at the door as it was pushed open and in walked Summer thick ass.

"I'm sorry. I didn't know you had company. I was just dropping this off anyway. I'm about to head to class."

"This nigga ain't company. Summer meet my little brother, TK. TK, this is my lady Summer." He turned to look at her then looked back at me kinda like he was shocked that my handsome ass pulled a bad ass bitch like her. "Is yo rude ass gone speak? I questioned.

"My bad, my bad. Look I'ma leave y'all lovebirds alone. I gotta get back to my shit anyway. I just wanted to drop you off one of my new pieces." He threw the coat over the couch and got up. "It was nice meeting you, Summer. You be careful too, my brother is a real piece of work, for real." He dapped me up and headed out the door.

"He didn't have to run off so fast," she stated.

Pulling her down on my lap, I wrapped my arms around her waist as she looked at me and smiled. I wanted to bend her ass over not giving a fuck about those kids in the other room.

"He wasn't talking about shit anyway. A nigga missed yo ass," I replied. "You have been busy as fuck since we got back. I need you to make some time for me real soon."

"I will as soon as I finish these tests then I'm all yours. I promise."

"It's cool, mama. Education before me any day. Thank you for the food though. Now get yo ass up so you won't be late for class. Call me when you make it."

Kissing me, she got up and left out the room. Walking over to the couch, I picked up what my little brother dropped off before I started eating. Looking it over this shit was cold-blooded for real. It was all black and had his logo on it. He has always been a flashy dresseing mother fucker. When we were coming up big bro Turk and I used to call his ass Dresser, like the dude from *The Five Heartbeats*. He would go and buy a new fit and come out the room to show mama. Our big brother Turk would yell out, *Sho em, Dresser!* He would walk out the room like he was the flyest nigga in the crib. We all would be rolling at his funky Fresh Prince looking ass.

Tossing it back down, I went back to my seat so that I could smash my food. It felt like my stomach was on my back like ole girl from Latoya Nicole's book *Love and War: A Hoover Gang Affair*.

SUMMER

Looking at my watch, I saw that I was almost late. I had to meet this girl for class so that she can get my notes for the last test that we have. I'm so glad this shit is almost over. I'm ready to walk across that stage and hope on the first flight out of this bitch. So, if Knight is really checking for me, then he gone have to be with this long-distance thang cause staying in Illinois anywhere is not an option for me.

Getting my keys off the kitchen counter, I then headed out the door. I have to meet her in Broadview, so it won't take that long to get there anyway.

"AY SUMMER!" I turned back around to see what mama was yelling for.

"What, ma?"

"Here, carry this to the alley before you go. I would have asked your brother Markell, but his ass ran out the door so fast that I didn't have time to stop him."

Going back up the steps, I grabbed the bag of trash and headed behind the house. I was pissed when I made it to the back and saw Markell's car parked back here already. His ugly ass could have taken this shit back here for mama. I'm about to cuss his ugly ass right out too, lazy ass fucker.

I threw the trash in the bin and walked up to his car.

BAM! BAM! BAM!

I banged on the window right when I walked up.

"OH MY GOD, I'M SORRY!" I screamed. Running back up to the front, I tried to get to my car as fast as I could.

"SUMMER, WAIT!" he yelled out, but I refused to stop and talk to him. "SUMMER!" he called out again. Taking a deep breath, I finally stopped and turned around to him.

"Please don't tell anyone what you saw."

"Are you serious? How crazy would I look telling someone I just saw my big brother in the alley sucking dick?"

"*SHH, SHH*, why are you yelling?"

"Markell, please just let me go. I have no problem with your life-style, but at least do that shit where people can't see you."

"You promise not to tell mama?"

"Nah, I ain't promising shit because when you walked in on me fucking Alex in high school, you ran and told mama real quick. I should do the same to you, but that shit ain't my business. What you do with your mouth and your ass is your business. Now I have to go. You take it easy, loose booty," I joked.

I really didn't care what he did, but shit take that shit to a room, better yet your own house. Why the fuck would you sit in an alley and suck dick, knowing crackheads like Ezell walk around this bitch all day long. Next thing you hear is, *Hey Markell back here sucking dick.* Real loud. I laughed to myself because I damn near wanted to ask his ass for some tips.

That nigga jaws were so sunken in you could tell he was taking that nigga soul. I should have yelled out *Get it biiiih!* But, I didn't wanna fuck up his flow. It seems like I did that shit anyway though.

I got in the car and looked in my rearview mirror as I drove off only to see this lil nigga switch back to his car.

Shaking that shit out of my head, I headed to Broadview to meet this girl.

After I met with Cindy to give her the papers, I went right to Marquise house. I couldn't hold this shit in any longer. I'm just like my cousin Toya, that bitch can't hold water to save her damn life.

"What's good, sis?" Quise asked.

"Auuuntiiiie!" MJ squealed, running up to me with open arms. "I missed you so, so much. Daddy is boring, and Tameka can't cook. I be faking like I be eating her food, but when she leaves, I run it to the trash can."

He thought that was funny obviously because he was killing himself laughing.

"Trust me, I know. I'ma tell Nanna to start bringing you breakfast by here every morning. How does that sound?"

"GRREAT!"

"You don't have to eat that nasty woman food anymore." I kissed him on his cheeks as he ran off to play.

"Oh hey, Tameka. I didn't see you sitting over there next to Marquise," I lied. I saw her ass but didn't care. "Marquise can you come outside I need to discuss some family business with you."

"I'm family too, Summer. You don't have to act like that with me," Tameka spoke up.

"Girl please, just cus I have my brother's blood running through me and you have his nut running down your throat does not make us related. That makes me his sister and you nasty." She sucked her teeth and sat back on the couch.

As soon as we stepped outside, I had to let it all out.

"BRUUUH! Tell me why I caught Markell sucking dick behind mama house." This nigga didn't even look shocked.

"Try catching him sucking dick in the kitchen. I been knowing that shit sis. Why you think I made his ass find his own spot. I ain't against that shit. I just ain't with that shit. That nigga had his thugged out boyfriend sitting on the stove, while he sucked his dick. I made that nigga get the hell out IMMEDIATELY."

"Ahh hell, here I am thinking I just spilled some tea. Let me take my ass home. Tell that bitch to take some cooking lessons while she's around here trying to be family, funky hoe."

"Man gone." He playfully pushed me as I jogged down the stairs.

❧ 7 ❧

DESIRE'

"Bihhh," was all I heard when I walked into Summer's crib.

Lately, her ass has been on cloud fucking nine. Knight ass must have really dropped the bomb ass dick off to her while they were in Vegas. She's been happy as hell, and I can't even front like I ain't happy for her ass and low key jealous at the same time. My guy Domano is straight hood. Ain't no lovie dovie shit with him. He is gone grab me by my hair and fuck me until my pussy is blowing out air to breath. I love his sexy ass though.

"Bitch, listen." Summer announced pulling my attention back towards her. "That got damn Knight is a beast, do you hear me, sis? Our little getaway was everything I needed to clear my head and refocus back on myself. I didn't realize how much I had been so focused on my sister until I stopped. For the past few weeks, it has been fuck Summer, it's all about finding out what happened to my sister. After talking to Marquise's stupid ass, he made me realize that some things are best left buried. I wanna know what happened, and then I don't wanna know what happened. Finding out her ass was a stripper was already too much for me."

"Yo ass on that pole was too much for me, sis. Who the fuck hit yo ass with those damn tomatoes though." I started cracking up laughing all over again. "That shit had me and Destiny on that nasty ass flo crinnn'."

"MARQUISE!" she squealed.

"Bitch, I know you fucking lying. Yo brother did not do you like that."

"I promise his dusty ass hit me for real. I was pissed off when I saw it was him. How bout this nigga knew Sunny was working at the club. Talking about she's a grown woman, and we were sheltering her."

"Well..." I stated with much hesitation. You have to think about the shit you say to Summer because she will pop yo ass in a minute. I had to learn that shit the hard way. I'm just now getting the color back in the spots she pulled skin from.

"Well, what bitch? Because all mama and daddy tried to do was make her life easy. So they gave her the world and made sure she didn't do nothing that would get her fucked up. Point obviously proven since she is dead now."

"I get it, him telling you guys what was going on might have saved her."

"Exactly."

"That damn club probably had my sister on all type of drugs just to make her feel comfortable enough to get out there and show her body like that."

"Ok. Ok. I don't want to ruin your vibe because you have been doing so well focusing on you." I was trying to switch up the conversation before it got way out of hand. "We need to have a girl's night to celebrate yo ass passing these tests and also popping that cherry again. I'm sure yo ass started bleeding after y'all fucked."

"Whatever bitch, it's been a while, but it wasn't that damn long. My gawd. He fucked all of the cum out of my ass and had a bitch walking like I was trying to hold my piss. My ass was scared to open my legs up all the way. I thought my damn uterus was gone slip out."

"He gave yo ass what you been missing."

"Right, now my ass can't stay off the dick. He got me running to take his ass lunch and wait for him to eat me for dessert."

"Y'all are too much. I'm about to go and see Domano ass so that I can get some money. Make sure you are ready by ten o'clock and wear something tight."

Leaving out of her house, I jumped in my car and headed straight to the block. Domano was always in the trap getting to the money, and I be thirsty to ride down on his ass and hit those pockets up.

"What's up, baby?" Domano asked as he approached my car.

"I missed you, daddy."

"Stop fronting, you know yo ass just came over here for some money. I already had it waiting on yo spoiled ass," he replied, handing the money to me through the window. "Aight now you know I don't like you around this shit. Call me later; I won't be out here all day. You still taking Summer out tonight?"

"Yea."

"Aight, here go a little more then. Y'all have fun and be safe. I'll be home to fuck the shit out yo sexy ass before you go though. I need that pussy to be smelling like cum, so it will keep the niggas away."

"Ha! Boy, get the hell back. You silly! I love you."

"Love yo crazy ass back, G," he replied and went back in the trap house.

Domano stood 6'3, 360 waves, sexy ass chocolate skin, and had a nice body with tattoos all over him. Since the first day I saw his ass, I knew I wanted him. I didn't step to him on no thirsty shit. When my sister told me he was at the store on the corner, I rushed my ass into my room and threw on some short ass jean shorts I cut off. They showed the bottom of my fat ass, and I threw on a crop top with it. I knew all it would take was for my ass to walk past him one time and it was over for any bitch he was fucking with before me. Domano's ass has been my dude ever since.

SUMMER

"Bitch, I hope Knight don't see yo ass in that little ass dress tonight. You ain't leaving shit to the imagination," Destiny stated as we walked out the house.

I wore this tight ass dress I got from Fashion Nova. It was all black, and the sides were out and only being held together by some lace. Of course, I couldn't wear panties with this because you would be able to see them, so a bitch is rocking nothing at all underneath.

"Girl, Knight has a business meeting, he will be occupied and by the time he comes over tonight, I will already be out of this. Besides he is not my damn daddy. We haven't made it official yet. Although he calls me his girl to everybody he introduces me to, we're just chilling. He's just a person who's knocking the dust off this pussy and who takes my mind away from a lot of other things."

"Yea, we will see," Destiny replied as we pulled up to the club.

The crowd was thick as hell, but sis got us VIP tables, so we went right in. We held hands and danced our way through the crowd to our section.

"Ayyye, this my shit!" Desire' yelled out as "No Limit" by G- Eazy and Cardi B started playing. "Fuck with me and get some money (ayye) Fuck with me and get some money."

She started doing her little twerk she like to do off every damn song as me and Destiny stood back and watched her. "Come on, sis. This is your night. Turn the fuck up bitch."

We started drinking before we came, so she was already fucked up when we walked in completely in her own zone and not giving a damn about her ass hanging out the bottom of her dress when she bent over.

The bottle girls came around and placed two bottles of Ace of Spade at our table. Not asking who sent them, we just started pouring up and dancing harder.

"Wanna go to the floor?" Destiny asked but before I could reply she was already snatching my ass down the stairs. I was so fucked up it felt like my body was moving slow to the music.

I heard Desire' yell out over the music, "Fuck it up, fuck it up!" followed by her crazy ass smacking me on my ass while I twerked to the music.

Feeling someone stand behind me, I looked back and saw this fine ass mother fucker just standing there waiting on me to start back twerking. He has his dick pressed so close to my ass that if I moved wrong, the shit might slip in. My dress started to rise, and I quickly pulled it back down before it exposed my naked ass. Feeling it rise again, I then noticed this nigga was pulling my shit up on purpose. Before I knew it, the nigga was dry humping my ass. Desire' and Destiny thought the shit was funny cause I was looking confused as fuck as I tried to move his hands from around my waist.

He pushed my body over, placing one hand on the back of my neck, keeping one hand on my waist as he pumped like his life depended on it.

"Nigga, get the fuck off me!" I yelled out. By this time I didn't think the shit was funny at all. Snatching away from him as hard as I could, I turned around and hit his ass right in the mouth. "I told yo ass to get the fuck off me!" I yelled over the music.

He looked at me and drew his hand back. Before he could get to me all the way, he was snatched back and thrown to the ground. All I saw was a black hoodie with a tiger face on the hood part. I was in total shock. Desire' tried to pull me away, but I had to see his face.

Remembering what my brother said he saw in the video of my sister leaving the club.

My heart was racing as the crowd started to scatter but not me.

"Bitch, let's go now."

"No wait, I have to see."

"Fuck that; we need to leave now, Summer." I noticed his body turned towards me quickly and the hood fell slightly off his face.

"TAKE YO ASS HOME, SUMMER!"

My eyes grew big as hell once I recognized the voice. Knight looked at me before standing up allowing the bouncers to snatch up the guy he was just beating. He started walking towards me as I frantically shook my head back and forth at him, not wanting him to get close to me.

"IT WAS YOU. YOU KILLED HER!" I yelled out. He looked at me confused and kept walking up on me.

Turning away, I grabbed Desire's hand and ran out of the club. Jumping into the car, my heart was racing, and tears started coming down. Just seeing him with that hoodie on fucked me up. I wanted to beat his ass. I wanted to yell at him and ask him why he lied to me. Now I see why he was trying to get my mind off my sister so fucking much.

"Come on, boo." Destiny stood by the door, reaching out for my hand to help me out of the backseat. "You sure you want to stay home by yourself?"

"Yes, I need to get my head together and call my brothers over."

"Can you tell us what's going on before you go inside?" Desire' requested. Thinking it over, it sounded like a good idea just in case this nigga tried to pop up at my shit.

"My brother watched the tape of the night my sister left the club. He didn't see the guy face just said he had on a black hoodie with a tiger face on the hood which was the exact same thing Knight had on tonight."

"Damn! You think he is the person that did this. Don't you think that could possibly be anybody? Last winter it was so many niggas out here looking like ghetto hood twins with that shit on. It made no damn sense."

"Oh, it's just a coincidence that the nigga is rocking the exact same thing. I think the fuck not. It has to be him."

"Or maybe you are so obsessed with finding the person that you are willing to accuse anybody."

"You know what, fuck you Des. Get the fuck off my doorstep, stupid bitch!" Slamming my door in her face, I instantly broke down crying on the floor.

BAM! BAM! BAM!

"SUMMER, OPEN THIS FUCKING DOOR!" I jumped up as I heard Knight's voice boom from the other side of the door. "OPEN THE DOOR BEFORE I BREAK THIS MOTHER FUCKER DOWN, FOR REAL, G! WE NEED TO FUCKING TALK."

"FUCK YOU KNIGHT, YOU WEAK ASS MOTHER FUCKER."

As soon as those words rolled off my tongue, my door was coming off the hinges. He rushed in before my ass could run and snatched my ass up quick as fuck. Swinging on him while he had me pinned to the wall, the more I hit him, the more I cried, and he started to kiss my tears away.

"Baby, talk to me and tell me what's wrong?"

"FUCK YOU!" I cried out and delivered a blow right to his jaw that dazed his ass.

Dropping me to the floor, I ran into my room and locked the door, which was the dumbest idea ever since I saw what he just did to my front door. Using his shoulder, he knocked the door down, and there I stood with my 9mm Marquise bought me. Pointing it right at his head, I nervously shook as he stood there with his hands up surrender style.

"WHY? JUST TELL ME WHY DID YOU DO IT?" I questioned, wiping the tears away from my face.

"I DIDN'T DO SHIT. NOW TALK TO ME LIKE A GROWN AS MOTHER FUCKING WOMAN AND STOP PLAYING THESE FUCKING GAMES!" he yelled and started walking up on me more.

Pulling the trigger, I allowed a bullet to hit the wall behind him.

"DON'T GET CLOSE TO ME. TELL ME WHY DID YOU KILL MY SISTER, KNIGHT. YOU CAME INTO MY LIFE

QUICK AND TRIED TO DO ALL YOU CAN TO GET MY
MIND OFF HER, OFF TRYING TO FIND OUT WHO DID
THIS SHIT WHEN IT WAS YOU THE WHOLE TIME."

"WHAT THE FUCK! SUMMER, DO YOU HEAR HOW
CRAZY YOU FUCKING SOUND. I DIDN'T KILL YOUR
SISTER. I DON'T KNOW WHAT THE FUCK HAPPENED TO
HER ASS, ALL I KNOW IS IT WASN'T ME."

"THE COAT YOU HAD ON WAS THE SAME COAT OF THE
GUY THAT SHE LEFT WITH."

Pinching the bridge of his nose, he tried to get himself to
calm down.

"Summer baby listen. This is the coat my brother dropped off to
show me the other day while you were there, it's a part of his collection. This is my first time wearing the coat, and I just threw it on cus it
was the first thing I saw. You know how the fucking temperature drops
here at night, so I just grabbed this and headed out to the meeting,
which was held in the back of the club yo ass was showing out in. You
have to believe me. I would never do anything to hurt you, and if she
were still alive, I wouldn't hurt her either. I was trying to get your mind
off her because I know how it can be to obsess over something
happening to a family member. Last year, we lost our other brother.
That fucked my little brother up the most, and for a while, he was
obsessed with finding out who killed him too.

Listen; lower the gun so that we can talk. You have to believe me. I
have too much going on to do some shit like this and for what
reason, ma?"

He was right, I had no proof that it was him and deep down I felt
like it wasn't him. Maybe Desire' was right. I had become so obsessed
with finding the person that I was willing to accuse anybody. Thinking
it over a little more, I decided to lower the gun as I dropped down to
my knees.

"It's ok, baby," he mumbled into my neck as he got down on his
knees and held me close to him. "All I wanna do is protect you and
make you happy shorty, that's it. I can't protect you if you are accusing
me of doing some shit I would never ever do."

He kissed me on my forehead before standing to his feet. Lifting me off the ground, he raised my dress above my head before going over to my dresser and pulling out my favorite nightgown I like to sleep in. Sliding it over my head, he started pulling my arms through the sleeves like my ass was a toddler and couldn't do it myself.

"Lay down. I'm going to call my guy over to fix your front door right now," he stated, and I did as I was told.

I laid in bed for about 30 minutes before he came back into the room. I rolled onto my back and watched him as he stripped down to his boxers and got under the covers with me. Not saying a word, he kissed me on the back of my neck and wrapped his arms around me.

"Get some rest, and we can talk about this more in the morning." I nodded my head yes with my face resting on his arm.

Laying here quietly as I listened to him snore while I tried to force myself to sleep. My mind was all over the place as I allowed my tears to roll down his arm onto my bedsheets. I started praying to God that he was really telling the truth. I still have plans on telling Marquise and Markell what happened so that they can figure this shit out because I'm about to run myself crazy.

8

KNIGHT

I woke up early as hell this morning and started cooking breakfast. I scrambled eggs, bacon, grits, and a nigga even flipped a few pancakes. I wanted to do whatever to make my lil baby happy again. Last night was fucked up for the both of us. I wanted her to go out and enjoy herself with her friends, but shit went left really quick. I'm not even sure how we ended up arguing about her thinking I killed her sister. That shit blew the fuck out of me because I would never do no shit like that. Maybe I have done some fucked up things in life but murdering someone is not it. Well... I take that back, murdering a female is not it. Now a nigga talking shit to me or fucking with my money can get bodied any day.

Placing her food on the tray, I poured some orange juice and added that to the side. She was in the room snoring loudly, so I already knew she was exhausted. Walking in the door-less room, I sat the food on her desk before walking to her bedside. Pulling the covers back, I stood there and admired her beautiful body. The nightgown I put on her last night was now above her waist exposing her soft ass.

My mouth started to water the more I looked at her, and I just had to get a taste. Climbing under the covers, I moved her juicy thigh over, so I could get a full view. I licked my lips before I pressed them against her lips, kissing them before I devoured her. I began nibbling softly on her lips until I used my hands to spread them apart. Once my eyes landed on her clit, I started sucking and slowly licking it, causing her to squirm.

"Hmmm!" she moaned out as her hands gravitated to my head. She started lifting her body off the bed to get away from me, but that only made me go harder. Wrapping my arms around her thighs, I pulled her to the middle of the bed.

"Don't run from me, baby," I mumbled. "Let it out, baby! Let me see that pussy cream."

"Ooooh shiiiii!" she screamed as her juices started flowing out. I sucked until her body was limp and she couldn't do nothing but lay there and shake. "Damn, boy."

"Nah baby, it's a grown man this way. Now get up so you can eat breakfast." I requested as I moved her tray over to the bed.

"You not gone eat?"

I cocked my head to the side before I replied, "I just did." She smacked her lips and laughed.

"Boy! I was not talking about that."

"Shit, that was the sweetest meal I had since we left Vegas." Taking a seat next to her, I was trying to decide if we should talk about last night or not. Her morning started out good, and I hate to ruin it over the bullshit from last night.

"Before you say anything, wash your face because my nut is starting to dry up around your lip. Yo ass is sitting over that looking like Dave Chappelle when he was acting like that crackhead. Looking like yo ass is about to start scratching and asking if I got any more of that nut over there." She started laughing hard as hell while stuffing pancakes in her mouth.

"Oh, my gaaaawd! Baby, these taste so much better than Meka's pancakes. Her shit tasted like she forgot the eggs, they didn't even rise. She had my brother over there eating hoecakes."

"The fuck is a hoecake."

"You know when yo mama or grandma makes cornbread, and they fry it like a pancake instead of baking it? It's called a hoecake."

"Nah bruh I ain't ever ate no fried cornbread. That's some hoe shit." She tossed the pillow at my head quickly.

"My granny ain't no hoe."

"Oh...ok," I stated, giving her that Waka Flocka GIF look.

I got up from the bed to go and wash my face before the nut gets stuck in my beard. I decided not to mention what happened last night. I'm just going to get her out the house and make her ass smile all day. I plan to show her ass I'm a good man, and she should take a chance on me. We've been together daily since we met, and I love every minute of the time spent.

Once we left for Vegas, I dropped all my old hoes and focused on her. When that tight pussy gripped my dick like thongs stuck in a big bitch ass, I knew she was the one for me. It was like her pussy put some of that New Orleans voodoo on me and had a nigga ready to ask her to marry me.

"I figured I would send you to my cousin Pajae shop, so you can get that bush fixed and then later we could go to dinner or something."

"That's cool, babe. I hope your cousin doesn't fuck my shit up. Ion like a lot of hoes in my head."

"Really! My cousin ain't no hoe."

"Neither is my grandmother, but that didn't stop you from calling her one," she replied quickly as she brushed past me with her empty plate. Leaning back from the door, I couldn't help but watch her gown cling to her ass. I had to grip my dick to calm his ass down.

"We can do what you have planned but first..." She paused and turned towards me. "I just want some dick."

Slipping the gown above her head, I felt my dick rock up, but this time wasn't no controlling him. He was in desperate need of feeling her and about to bust out my boxers trying to get to her.

"Don't just stare, bring dat ass her boi," she joked. Gesturing for me to come close to her with her finger, while she laid back on the bed. I dropped my boxers and started making love to my baby.

Summer has officially become my weakness. Anything she wants or needs I promise to give it to her with no hesitation. This may be too early to say, but I'ma make shorty my wife one day.

SUMMER

I had intentions on getting up early and going over to Marquise's house to talk to him about last night. That was until Knight woke me up to breakfast and head, making that thought slip my mind quickly. I didn't know what to do when his cock strong ass took the door off the fucking hinges. I didn't know if I wanted to run or fuck the shit out of him. That strong shit be turning my ass on. I wanted his ass to toss me around how he did that door and fuck me until the pain went away.

After he calmed me down and told me about the coat being a part of his brother collection, I felt stupid as hell. Ain't no telling who the fuck was wearing a coat like that. I'm starting to say fuck this shit. The police are not trying, so shit, why should I?

"What's on your mind?" he asked, pulling me from my thoughts.

"Nothing, baby," I replied, reaching over to rub the back of his head. "Just excited to see what all you have planned for us. We had so much fun in Vegas, so I already know you have some tricks up your sleeve."

"Absolutely, and we gone start with you getting that wig split first and then go from there. While you are waiting, I'm going to stop by my moms and holla at for her a minute." I nodded my head as I noticed we were coming to a stop. We pulled up to a house, and I immediately rolled my eyes.

"I know damn well you don't think I'm about to let someone do my hair out of their kitchen."

"If you don't get 'cho high maintenance ass out the car."

This mother fucker started laughing like he thought I was joking. He must not know I'm more serious than a nigga on Maury saying *He is not the father*.

"No, I'm not. I could have gotten my own hair done for the day. You should have told me she wasn't in a real shop. Does she even have a license? I go in with hair down my back and come out looking like Anna Mae when ole girl left her perm in too long. You got me fucked up, G!" I spat. Sitting firm in my seat, I folded up my arms, and I waited for his ass to pull the fuck off. I heard him open the door, so I yelled out to him.

"Yea that's right. Go and tell your cousin she has one less client head to fuck up tuh-day." My door swung open and I was lifted out and thrown over his shoulders. "Put me down Knight, for real this bitch is not about to Anna Mae my ass!" I yelled out.

"Man, if you don't shut the hell up," he replied hastily. We walked into the house and went right down to the basement.

Hearing house music playing and women laughing caused me to stop shouting. He lowered me to my feet and turned me around.

"Crazy ass, this is my cousin Pajae, Pajae, this is my crazy ass girl Summer."

Looking around the basement, I was shocked as hell. She had it set up just like a shop. She had her dryers on one side and her shampoo bowl on the other. It was two more booths there, and she stood at the third station finishing up a sew in.

"You happy now?" he whispered in my ear. "Her shit is legit, thanks to me."

"Hey hunny, I will be with you in a second. I'm almost done," she announced as she turned her client around to the back giving her a big mirror to look at her hair closely. I nodded my head ok and took a seat in her waiting area.

I ain't even gone front so much was going through my mind when this nigga started walking me down the stairs. I legit thought his ass was about to kill me like Sunny. I really need to get that out of my head before I run his ass away.

"I'm about to go. Call me when she's almost done so that I can head back over here. Make sure she doesn't Anna Mae yo ass."

"Oh gosh stop! I'm so embarrassed," I stated, covering my face up.

"Nah ya parents just sheltered your ass, and you don't know that some of the dopest shit is created in a basement. Except this, cause she gone fuck you up, for real." He turned away quickly and ran up the stairs. He better be joking, or I'm gone tear this basement up when she finishes. Let my head be fucked up. Ain't no mo shop bihh!

❧ 9 ❧

KNIGHT

I walked into my brother store so that I could have a conversation with him about last night. I told Summer I was going to my moms, but I didn't want her to think anything if I said my brother.

"What's good, big bruh?" TK stated as we dapped each other. "What brings you to the hood? You know yo ass don't partake in this shit no more."

Ok so, I lied a little bit. He not only owns a store and has a clothing line, but he also slangs more dope than El Chapo. At first, I was pissed when I finally found out what he was doing, especially since he saw them drag my ass off to prison. You would think that would scare him away from the shit.

"I wanted to ask you something, and I want you to be honest."

"Go head, bruh. What's on your mind?" He adjusted himself in his seat before firing up a blunt.

"You remember when you came by the office the other day. You looked at Summer than at me, what was all that about?"

"I was trying to see how yo uglass pulled her sexy ass. Shorty is too much woman for you.

"Man, whatever, I was just wondering though. Her sister got killed about a month ago, and the person she left the club with was wearing one of your hoodies."

"Damn, that's fucked up. As far as those coats, shit it was so many of those made that shit could have been anybody."

"I already know, bruh. I told her ain't no telling who had that coat cus that shit sold out when you first launched that line."

"Exactly! Anyway, I gotta cut this short though. I got a meeting with a buyer in 20 minutes."

"Aight G, you be safe."

"Always."

Leaving out of his office with a weight lifted off my shoulders. I was satisfied with his answers cus I would hate to hurt my little brother for doing something so fucking stupid.

"Yea," I said speaking through the phone when I saw Summer's name pop up.

"Don't yea me, nigga. It's yes ma'am," she joked.

"You funny! You ready, Anna Mae?"

"Fuck you, come pick me up."

After letting her know I would be there shortly, I swung by a store first to pick up something for her. Jumping back in my truck, I did the dash down the expressway, getting off on Mannheim. Pulling in front of my cousin crib, Summer was standing on the porch talking to her. She looked so fucking pretty. She's always pretty, but with her hair straight like that, she's gorgeous.

"I see she left you a little bit of hair," I announced when she slid her thick ass in my seats.

"Why you gotta be a hater? You just jealous cause my hair is longer than your mother's." She started laughing, but I damn near back handed shorty.

"Keep playing and you gone have to come back tomorrow once I fuck the shit out of yo ass tonight for talking about my mama. I don't wanna hear, *ohh fuck, Knight! That hurts baby, shit. Shit, slow down pleaaase!*" I mimicked her voice.

"Trust me, daddy. If I am saying all of that, I'm faking it." She winked at me, and I immediately pulled over on the side of the expressway. Getting out the car, I came around on her side and opened the door. "Boy, let's go. I'm not about to play with you."

"You about to play with this dick though." Turning her around to make her legs hang out of the door, I was happy as hell she had on a dress too. I could tell she was turned on because once I open her legs, I saw that pussy glistening. Pulling my dick out, I rammed it inside of her, putting as much of my body inside the truck. She was holding on to my neck for dear life and trying her best to hold back her moans.

"Talk that shit now, Summer."

"Hmm!" she moaned out and bit down on my shoulder.

"Nah, you had a lot to say about faking it, right." She wrapped her legs around me pulling me in closer to her.

"Right there baby, shit. I'm about to cum."

I pulled out and put my dick up as soon as she said that. Shorty had me all the way fucked up thinking I'm about to let her get a good nut after she said she be faking. She had better fake that damn nut and enjoy her fucking day.

SUMMER

I watched him put his dick up while I sit with a shocked look on my face. He thought that shit was funny, but I got a trick for his ass. Once he got in the truck, I started playing with my pussy. I was gone get this nut with or without his ass. He pulled off and could hardly keep his eyes on the road. When I felt my nut coming, I started rubbing my clit fast. I started squirting so hard that shit went flying to his front window. As soon as I finished, I grabbed a wipe out of my purse and cleaned myself up.

"You know you about to clean this shit up, right?"

"NOPE! All you had to do was let me cum, but nooo. You wanna play games and shit, so that was my payback. Now take me to my house so I can shower and get dressed for the day." He didn't say anything, but I could tell he was pissed off. I thought the shit was funny just like he did when he didn't let me finish.

"Where are we going?" I questioned, but he didn't answer me. After about 30 minutes, we pulled into an empty lot. He went inside and came back out with a bucket, a rag, and one of those window washers they use at the gas stations.

"Here," he said, handing me all the shit he had in his hand. "Clean that shit up so we can go have dinner."

"Knight you got me fucked up. I'm not about to clean that shit up. You better go find a crackhead and let them do that shit."

"I SAID CLEAN THE SHIT UP!"

"AND I SAID..." I stopped in the middle of my sentence when I saw he now had a gun pointed at me. "Are you serious?"

"As a mother fucking heart attack. Now hurry up because we have reservations at eight."

I couldn't do anything but shake my head at him. Just looking into his eyes, it's like he was zoned out and didn't care about me or nothing else. This isn't the person I met. Same as when he took my damn doors off the hinges. How can Knight go from this loving person who always wanted to see me laugh and smile to this dark person that I can't wait to get away from?

I got out the car and started cleaning the inside of his windows, not saying a word to him. He walked off on the phone, and I could just feel the tears filling up in my eyes. I was hurt because this nigga actually pulled a gun on me. I'M DONE once he takes me home.

I finished cleaning his window and sat back in the front seat, waiting for him to come back to the truck. He grabbed the supplies and took them back inside the warehouse. I just stared out of the window because if I were to say anything, I am bound to punch his ass in the throat.

You know what, maybe it's me. It's something about me that attracts the wrong mother fuckers. The last dude couldn't get his shit together, and this one here has a dark side that I obviously do not want to see. I'm going to pull myself together, focus on my last few weeks of school, and live for me. Fuck everything and everybody else.

This pussy is about to turn into a bush again all because of his crazy ass.

⊗⚬⊗

"He did what?" Destiny asked with her face full of sadness. "Knight does not seem like that type of person. I mean when he was younger yea, he had a quick ass temper, but shit people should grow out of shit like that."

"Yea you would think, huh. Once he took me back to my apartment, I grabbed me some change of clothes and dipped. He made reservations for us somewhere, but after that bullshit, I was not going anywhere with his crazy ass."

Tossing back my last drink, I decided to turn in for the night. I turned my Pandora on and let my Jasmine Sullivan station play. The first song that started to play was Jasmine Sullivan "Forever Doesn't Last". I rolled over on my side and forced myself to sleep.

છત્ર

The sun started shining in through the window, and all I could think about was how yesterday was finally over with.

"Good morning." I sat up in the bed quickly once I heard Knight's voice.

"How did you get in here?" I questioned with my heart racing because he scared the shit out of me.

"WHO THE FUCK BROKE MY DAMN DOOR?" I heard Desire' scream out.

"Summer, please just listen to me," Knight blurted out.

"Did you break the door?" I asked calmly.

"It was either the front door or come in through the window. I didn't want to scare you, so I thought the front door was more formal," he replied. He obviously thought that shit made a lot of damn sense.

"Summer, what the fuck? Did you see this shit?" Desire' asked as she was walking back down the hall. Once her eyes landed on Knight, she stopped at the door. "You want me to call the police to get his crazy ass out of here?"

"NO DES DON'T. I'll get the door fixed. I just really needed to talk to Summer."

"Well, you better talk fast because after yesterday I really don't have shit to say to you. You really pulled a fucking gun on me. How is it ok for you to play with me, but when I play back then it's an issue? You got mad like I squirted in your face or some shit." My mouth was running so fast that I wasn't even giving him a chance to speak.

"You gone let me talk?"

"Nah, because nothing can take back what you did, so there is nothing else left for us to talk about. Now, call your boy to fix they door, and you can go about your business. I'm good on you." He looked at me while biting his bottom lip.

"Just let me."

"NO!" I blurted out, cutting him off. "You can just leave." Getting up out of the chair he was sitting in beside the bed, he turned to look at me then walked out of the door.

"Someone will be here in a minute to repair your door. Sorry about that," he said to Destiny and Des who were now standing in the doorway with their arms folded up.

10

MARQUISE

"Daddy, daddy, daddy!" MJ called out to me as he and Tameka walked back in from the store. "Look what Tameka got me?" He pulled a big ass bag of hot Takis out and waved them back and forth at me.

"That's good, but you know you can't eat those, right?"

"But whyyy?" he whined.

"First, because I said so and that should've been the end of it. Secondly, because they are too damn hot, son. I don't even know who would give a four-year-old these hot ass thing anyway."

"Tameka," he replied like I was really looking for an answer.

"Go to your room and watch a movie. I'm about to talk to Tameka for a second and then I'll be in there to join you. Ok?"

"Ok, dad." He grabbed his juice and ran out of the living room.

I looked to make sure his door was closed all the way before I went into the kitchen with Tameka. Hearing the door shut, I grabbed the big ass bag of Takis and stormed into the kitchen.

I threw the bag at her, hitting her on the side of the head.

"What the fuck?" she spat.

"Why the fuck would you buy my son those hot ass chips? He's fucking four years old, and you thought that was the smart thing to do. You gone have my son asshole burning and shit."

"The fuck he asked for them for if he couldn't eat them?" I pinched the bridge of my nose so that I could calm down.

"He probably asked because he saw he was with a dense bitch and realized he could get away with asking. You never see me give my son nothing hot like this, Tameka."

"Did you hear the keyword you said? Your son. He asked for them and who am I to tell him no?" She shrugged her shoulders like she could give a damn.

Now granted, he's not hers, and I get that, but she's been around him since he was a baby. She should want the best for him as well, or so I fucking thought. I was heated for real, and it's taking everything in me not to knock her head against the microwave. She's lucky I don't hit bitches.

"You know what? I'm tripping. MJ should have known he was not supposed to eat these. I'll deal with him later but let me deal with you right now." Wrapping my arms around her waist, I started kissing her on the back of her neck. "I'm sorry for yelling at you and hitting you in the head."

"It's cool, baby," she replied while turning around to face me. She wrapped her arms around my shoulders and started kissing me aggressively, and I knew then she was ready to fuck.

"Go in the room and get naked for me. I'ma check in on MJ and then I'll be in there."

"Yes daddy, hurry yo ass up too."

"Aye, grab the Takis," I threw over my shoulder as I walked down the hall to MJ's room.

"Ooooh shiiit let me find out you on some freaky shit," she said as she grabbed the chips and switched hard to the bedroom.

After making sure he was good, I closed his door and went back down the hall to my bedroom. Tameka was laying in the bed butt naked playing in her pussy.

"Just like that, baby," I stated as I watched her do everything to get her pussy wet. She was sucking her fingers and then putting it in her pussy repeatedly. Shaking my head, I damn near wanted to laugh at her cause she was trying hard too.

"Turn over for daddy. I got something that will get you nice and wet, oh and let's not forget HOT." She jumped up quickly and got on all fours and put the perfect arch in her back. I started rubbing my finger up and down the slit of her pussy.

"Spread your ass cheeks for daddy."

She did as she was told and waited impatiently for me to start sucking her clit from the back. Daddy had another surprise for her tonight though. I smacked her on her ass before I palmed it and gave it a jiggle. I started playing in the little juices that she managed to make come down. As I played with her clit, I spit on her asshole and slowing put my thumb inside. Tameka like freaky shit like that, so I knew she wouldn't stop me. Once I saw she was nice and ready, I removed my finger and started inserting hot Takis into her asshole.

After I pushed about four to five in, she finally asked me, "Hmm baby, you brought us some new toys? This one is a little rough, but I like it." Arching her back more, she began to moan after every chip I inserted.

"Yea ma, I got something that will make your ass sweat. Maybe then the juices will leak down into that dry ass pussy of yours."

I don't know what happened, but shorty pussy used to get wet if the wind blew hard, so I don't know why all of a sudden the shit just stopped.

"Wait, wait. MARQUISE, THIS SHIT IS BURNING!" She jumped up quickly squeezing her ass cheeks together. She noticed the redness on my fingers and the opened bag of Takis.

"I KNOW DAMN WELL…" Before she could finish her sentence, she was running to the bathroom trying to get her asshole to stop burning. I know one thing; she ain't getting those chips out. I push them things so far up her ass they probably swimming around in her uterus.

"WHHHHY?" she cried out."

"You didn't care about my son ass burning so ion care about yo shit. Get yo shit and get the fuck out my house, dumb ass broad."

"Quise, I gotta get this shit out, it's burning my ass too bad."

"Did you hear that keyword you said? Yo ass! So that means that's not my problem. Now I said get your shit and get the fuck out." She got off the toilet clinching her ass cheeks together.

"Fuck you, you stupid mother fucker. You gotta be fucking retarded to do some shit like this. Who the fuck sticks chips up a bitch ass?" She slung her coat on with some leggings, and she stormed out of the house.

As she was running out, Summer was walking in.

"What the hell is stuck up her ass? She rolled her eyes at me like I did the shit to her."

"Man, fuck her!" I blurted out, waving her off. "What's good with you though?"

"I came to pick up MJ, he just Face Timed me and said Tameka needs help. Well... his exact words were. *TéTé, Tameka is in daddy's room crying and screaming saying her ass is burning.* That's why I asked what was stuck up her ass."

"His little nosy ass." I laughed. His little ass is always eavesdropping. "Go in there and get him. I got some shit to do at the club anyway."

"So, you actually own the club too? You know the one Sunny worked at."

"Yea, I thought I told you that. That's how she got the job there. I know the situation is fucked up, but lil sis was bringing in crazy money. When she started dancing the club would be packed as hell. To me, it was a win-win situation. She got her freedom and money that she has always wanted. As for us, we got more business that brought in a lot of money."

"Too bad she ended up losing in the end. She must have had her a real-life Myron on her hands."

"What you mean by that?"

"You know how dude used to make sure Diamond got home every night. He became obsessed with her in and outside of the club."

"Ion know about all of that. Like I said the only thing the tape showed was a black hoodie with a tiger face on the hood. Oh, and it had red diamonds as the eyes or rhinestone.

I just found out your boy Knight is part owner as well."

Once I saw him walk into the club, that nigga was talking my head off about Summer. I don't know what sis did to him, but his nose is wide the fuck open. Usually, I don't associate with the niggas she fucks with, mostly because my head is hotter than Tameka's ass. The first time Summer come home crying I be ready to bury a nigga.

Being the big brother I am, I picked up on how her attitude switched up when I mentioned his name. I won't ask her what's the issue, but I will ask him. Females have a tendency to tell one side, which is the fucked-up side of a man. So I'ma give this lil nigga the benefit of the doubt.

"Oh ok that's cool," was all she said and shrugged her shoulders. "I'll just get MJ and let you go about your business. I'm not doing anything tonight, so he can spend the night."

We left out the room and got MJ bags packed. I was happy as hell to finally get a break. Being a single father can be rough at times, especially having a bitch like Tameka's as a girl. She wasn't trying to do shit extra for MJ, and that shit showed on a regular.

SUMMER

Once I got Marquise Jr. buckled in, we headed straight to the Shedd Aquarium. I haven't been in this place since I was younger, and this will be his first time going. Once we finally found parking close enough to walk, we got out and headed inside. His little eyes lit up like it was Christmas when we made it all the way in. He wanted to run around and see everything. I was happy that I put on something comfortable because his little ass is on ten right now.

I watched him closely as he moved from one area to the next with me right on his heels.

"TeTe Summer, look!" he yelled out excitedly as he ran over to look at the sea lions. Pulling out my phone, I started recording his reaction and taking pictures to send to Marquise.

"What are those?" I quizzed.

"Sea lions, TeTe," he replied with a big smile on his face.

"Come on. Let's go this way so we can see the rest of the animals."

"Yes, ma'am."

Grabbing his hand, we walked over to the next area. When we made it further around my eyes locked with this guy I dated back in high school. Alex was and from the looks of him now, still is the sexiest mother fucker alive. He stood 5'11, light skin, clean cut mustache, perfect smile and he always smelled good as hell. His parents were both dentists, so they made sure all their kids had the world greatest teeth.

When we finished high school he moved away, so we just ended things. Well, he didn't just up and leave but him having a full scholarship to Louisiana State University for academics and football had a lot to do with it. I was hurt for real. Alex was my first everything. My first kiss, my love, and the first nigga I popped this pussy on. You know how most boys from high school be fine as hell then when they get older, and you see them they be ugly as hell.

Make yo ass put on the *OH NO LIL BABY WHAT WAS I THINKING* face but not Alex. Just looking at him now made me want to *slob on his knob like corn on the cob. Check in with me and do your job. Lay on the bed and give me head, don't have to ask don't have to beg.* Ayyye, my bad y'all. I always get caught up on that part.

"Summer?" Feeling a tap on my shoulder, I turned around and there his sexy ass stood making the floodgates open.

"Alex? Oh my gosh, what are you doing here?"

"I'm actually here with my wife Dawn and our little boy AJ." Annnd just like that my pussy dried up. Alex is married, Knight is a mini Hulk, I see now that a bitch just can't win for losing.

"I'm here with my nephew." I turned around to show him MJ. "Well, he was right here." I started looking around. "I'm sorry, I have to go." Running off, I started checking everywhere. In every little crack I saw.

"MJ... MJ! SWEETIE, WHERE ARE YOU?" I called out to him.

"TeTe Summer, I'm right here!" Hearing his little voice caused me to immediately spin around on my heels. "Can I get in too, TeTe?" he asked pointing at the diver that was in the shark tank feeding them.

"Didn't your father show you the video of the little boy getting dragged by Harumbe? A sweet little boy like you would be dessert for a shark. We leave things like that to the other color people."

"You mean white people, Te Te? Aren't I white?" he stated in a serious firm tone. My brother is a bright yellow, and MJ took all of his color; he may be a bit brighter.

"No, you're bright, there's a difference. Now come on before ya little ass run off again." Grabbing him by his hand, we headed towards the door. We are going to have lunch then I'm taking his inquisitive ass straight to mama house.

"Wait, Summer." Alex came towards me. For this nigga to have a wife he sholl ain't with her ass. I stopped so that he could catch up to us. "I leave back out in a few days, and I wanted to see if we can possibly do lunch and catch up."

"Umm nah I don't think that's a good idea. I'm sure your wife wouldn't like you going out to lunch with your ex," I replied, pointing towards the woman and child only a few feet behind him.

"That's not my wife. That's my cousin; she has been watching my son for me. She wanted to come along, so I brought her here with me. Just say yes and let me worry about my wife." I was a little hesitant, but he started giving me the puppy dog eyes and made a bitch lose my train of thought. I'm telling you now if I fuck him, it's not my fault. It's his for being so damn irresistible.

Even though I may regret this later, I decided to say yes anyway. One little meal won't hurt... right?

11

SUMMER

"Fuuuuck!" I moaned through clenched teeth as Alex pushed the rest of his thick dick inside of me.

We decided to meet up at his brother's house in Westchester before heading to Outback for lunch. I tried to wear less of *fuck my lace front loose* and more of *don't suck my whole soul out my pussy*. So, my outfit of choice was this navy blue and light blue tie-dye sleeveless sundress. It was very clingy, so it made my curves pop even more. Alex wasted no time snatching my dress up when I got inside the house.

I wanted to push him away, but the shit was feeling so good. The more we kissed, the more my feelings came rushing back.

"Wait... Alex!" I stated, trying to stop him. "Your wife!" I whispered. I was so caught up in myself that I forgot about her. I would hate for a bitch to be fucking my man while I'm at home playing with our son.

Breathing heavily while still thrusting inside of me and kissing on my neck, he said "She's dying, Summer. Please don't stop me; I really need you right now." My mind was all over the place at that moment. I didn't know whether I should feel sorry for her or myself since he's using me for the nut because she can't give it to him.

Pushing him out of me, I stood up quickly and pulled my dress down.

"I should go." I looked at him as he shook his head, took the condom off and pulled his pants back up. "I'm sorry, I just couldn't. This isn't right on any level. I know something is going on with your wife, but you should be there for her not here fucking me silly."

"I've missed you, and I just had to feel you again. I apologize for putting you in a situation like this. I know it had to be hard for you to say no to me. You've always been crazy about the dick and judging by the scratches I feel burning on my back, you still are."

Reaching for my hand, we went into the living room and sat down. I excused myself to the bathroom to freshen up, and once I finished, I came back out.

He was now sitting on the couch with drinks on the coffee table.

"Come sit," he said, patting the couch cushion next to him. Taking a seat next to him, I reached for the glass of red Kool-Aid and adjusted myself on the couch. "I should have told you about my wife, you know about her being sick and everything. Last year she found out she has lung cancer, and it's really taking a toll on her. She doesn't have that long left, so we decided to come back to Chicago to let her visit her family.

Things have been rough for us, I'm juggling my businesses, our son AJ, and taking care of her medical bills. It's a lot for real. When I saw you, my old life came back, and I kind of forgot about everything else. I just wanted to be back in my safe place, in my happy place, and your pussy always made a nigga feel better."

I wasn't sure if I wanted to be happy cause he said my pussy was the bomb, or if I should feel bad because that's all he thought of when he saw me. Bomb ass niggas.

"I hate that she's going through that, and I hate that you are stressing. I really hope things get better for you both. I can't be the one to make it right for you though. When I saw you, every feeling that I forced to go away when you moved away, was coming back. But you, when you saw me, you only saw my pussy as your happy place nothing else. No real feelings came back, you just simply wanted to get your dick wet."

Placing the cup back on the table, I stood up and gathered my things. A bitch was hungry as hell, but I'll take myself out before I eat with him only so he can get his nut later. I'm good, and I'll go back to not fucking before I let another nigga suck me in so quickly. Leaning down, I kissed him on the cheek and turned to walk away.

Before I took one step, the door was coming off the hinges. I rubbed my hand over my face in frustration.

"Nigga what the fuck? what is with you and knocking?" I yelled out to Knight as he stood there looking crazy.

"I just wanna talk, Summer."

"Yo, my nigga, what the fuck you do to my door?" Alex asked as he came over to my side.

"Look you Swiss Beats wanna be, I'm here to talk to my girl. I advise you to go back and be a blended family with Alicia and leave us alone."

"Oh, she's yo girl now, but she was a single bitch when I was just deep in those gu..."

Before he got that last word out, Knight had knocked his ass out. I wanted to run to the other side of the house where he landed and say, *you got knocked the fuck out, man.* But, I had to keep my attitude, so I laughed at his bitch ass on the inside. Looking back towards Knight, I walked through the opening where the door once stood and headed down the stairs. If I didn't think he was crazy before, I most definitely think it now.

"Damn, I can't get no conversation, Summer?" I turned around to face him as he hustled off the porch to catch up with me.

"Talk, go head. You got two minutes, and I'm gone." Looking down at my navy-blue Fossil watch, I made sure he knew that I was not playing.

"Not here, come back to my place or let's have dinner."

"Nah, I can't do dinner with no more niggas cause you mother fuckers feel like you should be tipped in pussy, obviously."

"I'm sorry, Summer. I should have..."

I threw my hand in his face to stop him from talking. "Times up," I hissed.

Turning away from him, I power walked to my car, jumped in, and sped the fuck off. Looking in my rearview mirror, my mouth dropped open cause this nigga was holding on to my bumper.

KNIGHT

I was leaving my boy Skillz crib when I saw Summer get out her car across the street. She had this tight ass dress on that she knows I wouldn't approve of unless her ass was with me. I haven't seen her in a few days, and she refuses for me to say anything to her ass. Like she only listens when you take the damn door off the hinges.

I know the way I reacted to her ass squirting on my window was fucked up. Her doing the shit was worse than my reaction. That's like me sending her to my cousin shop and nutting in her hair as soon as she came outside. All in all, it's a wasted nut. That shit could have been on my dick as I knocked her lil bow legged ass legs straight.

I still could have handled the shit differently though, but my anger got the best of me. Ever since I was younger, I had a temper problem. Just like most kids with fucked up attitudes, it was because of the shit that was going on at home. We used to watch our father beat the hell out of our mother. He would make us sit there in the living room while he used her as a fucking punching bag. He told us this is the only way you gain respect from a woman. If she steps out of line, beat her ass back in it until she starts requesting to be the line leader, like a First Grader. For an eight-year-old little boy, that was the worst thing you could ever see.

All we wanted to do was protect our mother, but he dared us to move or even say anything. I would sit there and think of all the different ways that I could kill him. Every time he did the shit, I would zone out, and it felt like a dark cloud would come over me. One time when the darkness came something clicked, and so did I. At this time, I was ten years old, and I had seen enough of the beatings.

As soon as he turned his back on us and walked towards our mother, I jumped up and lit into his ass. Every piece of strength I could pull up I was knocking his ass down. We went toe to toe, and he no longer looked at me as his child. He started beating me worse than he ever did our mother.

One good two-piece to the face dazed his ass. Before I could start back hitting him while he was down, my older brother intervened and sent two bullets through his head.

My father made me the animal I am today. After getting into so many fights and expelled from school, I had to learn how to keep the beast concealed. That's only until I really had to fuck a mother fucker up. Judging by the dude that just opened the door for Summer, I already know this shit won't be concealed for long.

Sitting in my car, I rolled up a blunt and waited to see how long she would be inside. I tried hard to wait on her to come out so that we could talk. After waiting about 30 minutes, I threw caution to the wind and got out the car. I had good intentions on knocking this time, you know before I let myself in. I saw the curtains were pulled back, so I looked through the window. Not expecting to see her leaning down to kiss him, I got pissed.

Stepping back a little, I did what I do best— took the mother fucking door off the hinges. I kicked that bitch one time, and the door blew back like an unsecured wig.

I was beyond pissed, but I couldn't show her because that's how I got myself in this situation in the first place. So here I am now, holding on for dear life to her bumper, just waiting for her to make a sharp right like they do in the movies and send my ass flying down Eastern Avenue. After about five blocks, scraped up knees and smoke from her muffler covering my face, she finally came to a stop.

"Get in the car!" she yelled out the window. Getting up off the ground, I got in the car, and the first thing she did was start laughing. "You know you crazy, right?"

"Only about you?" I stated, winking at her. She blushed and started back driving. Now I'm starting to think her ass is crazy too.

We pulled up to her apartment and went inside. She went into the kitchen and started pulling down pots and pans as I stood in the doorway and watched.

"You gone stand there and watch me or go clean yourself up so we can eat? The peroxide is under the cabinet. Judging by the blood stains that are on your knees, you are gone need the whole bottle."

"Shit, to be honest, I was gone slide this dick in you before we both did anything."

"Knight, if you don't go and wash yo ass," she joked, throwing a wet piece of lettuce at me, that she had just rinsed off.

Leaving the doorway I went into the bathroom and started cleaning up. The water from the shower was tearing my damn skinned knees up. I couldn't do shit but laugh at my big grown ass doing that shit anyway.

Closing my eyes, I stood under the water in the shower. Feeling my dick being massaged, I opened my eyes just in time to see Summer sliding my dick down her throat.

SUMMER

My crazy ass was forgetting that Alex just had this pussy stretched open from here to Calumet City less than an hour ago. I decided to stop preparing food and get in the shower with him. Even though we didn't fuck long, and I didn't cum, I'm pretty sure my pussy still smelled like used earring backs and Play-Doh from the condom that he wore.

Pulling my dress off, I pulled the shower curtain back and stepped in with him. I had intentions of stepping in and showering immediately, but his dick was bricked up when I got in. There's no way I could let a hard dick go to waste.

While he had his eyes closed, I dropped down to my knees before him, using one hand to take him into my mouth. I then grabbed a towel to clean my coochie with my free hand. He was not about to catch my ass slipping. I was sucking his dick and stroking him at the same time. The shit had to have been feeling good to him because I heard his toes popping over the water. Grabbing my head, he starts to slowly fuck my face. The longer he fucked my face, the longer I cleaned my pussy, because he was definitely getting this work when we got out the shower.

"Fuuuck!" he moaned out.

Unable to control himself any longer, he pulled me up, turned me around and placed my feet on solid grounds. *Everything that happened to me that was good, God did it.* My bad, these songs be taken over my thoughts sometimes.

Anyway, he pulled me up, turned me around, and started rubbing my pussy from the back. Once he saw that I was slippery enough to enter, he wasted no time sliding inside of me. I moaned out in pleasure because this shit was feeling so good. Alex's dick was big, but Knight's dick is big and thick with a curve. He got that dick that you can leave out the house, go around the corner, and it could still be inside you.

Gripping his dick with my pussy had him ready to cum already. He pulled out, slapped his dick against my ass cheeks a few times then went in for the kill, pounding himself in and out of me, making my head hit the wall. A bitch was almost light-headed until he lifted me up and slid me down on his dick.

"Right there, baby," I hissed. He started sucking on my breasts with a tight hold around my waist with his arms.

"This my pussy Summer!"

"Yes baby, it's yours. Shiiit!" I replied.

"I wasn't asking!" Right when those words slipped out of his mouth, his nut slipped out of his dick covering the inside of my walls. He was stroking me deep and slow, hitting my spot and I came right along with him.

Lowering me to the floor, we both washed up and got out the shower. I dried my body off and got right in the bed. I was gonna cook, but a bitch needed to get the feeling back in her legs first. Watching as he dried off, he then got under the covers with me. As he wrapped his arms around me, I pushed myself closer to his body.

"Why did you react like that the other day? It was like you had flipped just like that, and you had to know I was only joking with you. I could have gotten really mad because you pulled out in the middle of my nut, but I didn't. You wanted to play games, so I did the same. If I had known it would cause that type of reaction, I wouldn't have done it." He started rubbing my hair and planting several kisses on the back of my neck.

"As a child, I've seen a lot of abuse from my father. At first, I didn't know how to control my emotions, and I would flip the fuck out. As I got older, I learned just to keep quiet because things can go from zero to one thousand real quick. That's why I didn't say anything. I just shut down. I was wrong for making you clean yo piss up, and I really do apologize."

"It was nut, not piss." I added.

"Don't shit come out like that but piss baby girl. Anyway, I never want to see you hurt or upset because of me. I know what pain like that can do to a woman.

Hell, I know what pain like that can do to a child. We watched our father beat our mother so many times that it affected all of us. I became a hothead because for years I had to watch him do that shit, and I had to suck that shit up and not react to him. Once he was killed, I never held back my emotions again, and that didn't make shit any better for me.

My brother Tristan internalized it all, but our older brother, Turk, became just like our father. He used to beat the hell out of his girls, and for some reason, I would be the only one that could stop him. I remember this one time I was almost too late to stop him.

I was coming down the stairs of our parents' house as I wiped the sleep from my eyes. The closer I got to the bottom step the louder the screams became. I started running from room to room thinking my father was hurting my mother. I knew those screams all too well, but then I remembered my father was dead already. After checking my mother's room, I noticed she wasn't in there. Rushing back down the hallway, I still heard the screams, but I didn't see anyone.

Hearing them again, I realized the screams were coming from the basement but now they are getting weaker. Running down the basement stairs, my eyes were not prepared for what I saw. Turk had beaten his girlfriend so bad her face was unrecognizable. You could tell she was fighting him to stop because he had her handprints of blood over his shirt. Looking at her now, she no longer had any fight in her.

"Turk!" I yelled out, trying to get his attention, but just like me, he had already zoned out. I ran over to him and grabbed his arm in mid-swing. When he turned to me, his eyes looked dark as night. "STOP!" I said calmly. "You're going to kill her."

He looked from me to her and then back at me. His eyes slowly started to

turn back as the tears filled up in them. Looking back at her again, he then real-
ized what he had done. She had blood spilling out of the cuts in her face, and she
was already turning black and blue from the bruises. He picked her up and ran
out of the house, rushing her all the way to the hospital.

He had to do three years behind that, and she no longer talked to his ass again. He reached out to her several times and even had me telling her about his past. She wasn't hearing that shit though, and honestly, I didn't blame her. She was stronger than my mother, and I admired that about her. She had the strength to walk away the first time he hit her. Not my mother, she stayed and took the abuse because she was too busy worrying about not being able to take care of three kids on her own. That wasn't the first time my brother hit a girl, and even after him going to prison, it wasn't the last."

"Wow, I know that was tough to see. You gotta be better than that though. I will be damned if we have an argument one day and my ass wake up dead," I joked, and surprisingly, his ass actually laughed too. With him opening up to me, it really helped me see the real him. Not that the shit will ever make his actions ok, but just to know where all of it originated from helps.

After feeling my energy coming back, I kissed him on the cheek, and got out of bed. I then headed back into the kitchen to finish preparing dinner. For some reason this felt different with him, in a good way. I can't say where we might end up in the long run but for now, I'm willing to do what I have to do to fix his mentally disturbed ass.

❧ 12 ❧

DESIRE'

"Ο ne time for the birthday biiitch!" I yelled out as I walked into the backyard of my parents' house. They were having me a bar-b-que, and all of my friends and family were here. We have plans to go out later tonight, but right now, it's family time.

"HAPPY BIRTHDAY, BESSSTIE!" Summer squealed as she walked into the backyard with Knight walking in right behind her. I thought they fell off, but hey, as long as she's good, I'm good. That nigga just better not take any more doors off the hinges.

"Thank you, boo," I replied, reaching for a hug and that big ass bag she had in her hand. "For me?"

"Duh bitch, who else?" Snatching the bag from her, I started digging inside. Pulling out a box, I scrambled to open it. It was the Apple watch my ass have been saying I wanted for the longest. The smile grew wider on my face when she told me to keep looking. Shit that watch was enough for me, but a bitch gone keep digging. Looking up at her once I pulled the purse out of the bag, I yelled, "BITCH, YOU DID NOT BUY ME A FUCKING CHLOE' BAG?"

Rushing over to her, I gave her a tight ass hug. I was happy as fuck, I have been wanting this Chloe' shoulder bag for the longest, but I was not about to pay no damn $1,950 for it. She got the exact color I wanted too.

"You like it?"

"Bitch, I love it. Don't expect me to spend the same amount of money on you. Ion know how you did it, but thank you boo."

Walking back inside the house, I put my things up and headed back outside. Everybody was chilling, drinking, and having a good time. My father was on the grill, and I couldn't stop stealing pieces of his rip tips.

"Hurry up, daddy. I'm hungry."

"You better go inside and grab a hot link and wait on the rest. Yo ass ain't that got damn hungry."

Laughing at him, I stole another piece before walking away. I turned my attention towards the back gate right as Domano was walking in. My pussy started fighting to get out of these jeans I had on. He was looking so damn sexy.

"Damn Zaddy, I know you didn't come here empty-handed, right?"

"You know daddy always got that long dick for you. That's better than anything money can buy. Let's go in the basement and let me taste it."

Frowning up at him, I was getting irritated because I could smell the liquor on his breath. I should have known he was drunk the way he staggered in here. He was still looking sexy ass fuck, so I overlooked that shit. That was until he started making a scene and shit.

"No, I'm good, and you need to go home and sleep that shit off."

Pushing always from him, I was quickly snatched back by my arm. I turned around and started swinging on him. I didn't have to swing much because before I knew it, Knight, Marquise, and my brother Dee was all over his ass. I stood back and watched them stomp his ass. Not even bothering to stop them, I turned away and walked right back over to my daddy and stole another piece of meat.

"You already know Dee never liked Domano ass, so I don't even see why you invited him," Destiny added after daddy put his input in as well. They were really bugging. All Domano did was break my leg once and gave me two STDs, but shit they were curable, so I don't see what everyone else was so worked up about. After today, I am completely done with his ass though.

I sat back and watched them carry his ass off. He was so fucking drunk he probably didn't even feel the shit.

"Foods ready!" my dad yelled out, and we all ran to the table how they did on *Boyz n the Hood*. Everybody started fixing they plates like they just didn't beat somebody ass.

We ate and started drinking some more before the girls and I went back to our apartment to start getting ready to go out tonight.

⚜

"Sooo, what's going on with you and Knight? The last time we heard about him you called this nigga all types of crazy. You damn near said he was half of an inch away from being batshit crazy like Sunny." Stopping as soon as I realized what I had said, I looked up at her, and all I could think about was, *fuck she about to take her gifts back.*

"I'm so, so sorry, Summer, that slipped out. I didn't mean any—"

"It's ok," she stated, cutting me off. "You just had a little too much to drink that's all, we all have. Let's start getting dressed before you end up just like my sister, Sunny." Standing up to her feet, she started walking out the room. "Dead," she threw over her shoulder, and that sent a chill down my spine.

I waited until she was in Destiny's bathroom before I went into mine. My ass may be drunk, but I ain't crazy. I started washing up my body and my hair. I had decided on wearing it in its natural state tonight. Getting out the shower, I diffused my hair before heading out of the bathroom.

Turning my music on to the max while I got dressed, my song started playing by Tammy Rivera "Only One", so I start singing along. Pulling my black body dress out of the closet, I paired it with the purse that Summer just bought me with the Jessica Simpson pumps Destiny bought me for Christmas. Spinning around on my heels, I started singing with my eyes closed cause I was really feeling this shit.

"I might do my thing, I might, just might do my thing might take off this diamond ring and you bet not say nothing. Don't say shiiit to me, cause baby boy

ina fucking minute you gone be history, are you kidding me. Cause real soon you gone see what dem hoes bout, hope you like living at dem hoes house, cause I'm about to throw all yo clothes out."

BAM!

Stumbling back into the closet, I looked up and saw Summer standing there. "I told yo ass the last time that you will never disrespect my sister like that in front of me again." That was the last thing I heard before everything faded to black.

SUMMER

Closing the door behind me, I turned and bumped right into Destiny.

"I'm ready when y'all are," Destiny stated.

She wore this hunter green, tight fitted dress that had a gold zipper running down the back of it. The front was cut in a V, and she paired it with some hunter green peep toe, slip on ankle booties.

"I'm ready. Desire' had a little too much to drink, so she decided not to go out tonight. She was just up throwing up something terrible. I gave her water and an aspirin, and she went to sleep."

"Ahh damn, maybe I should check on her or stay home with her."

"NO! Girl please, we are already dressed, and she insisted on us going without her." She finally agreed to us leaving, so we grabbed our bags and headed out the door.

Fuck Des'. I told her she had one more time and apparently she thought shit was sweet.

"I hate she's going to miss us turning up for her birthday."

"I know right, cause we about to have a blast bitch. Des' was so damn dazed though; it's like the headache hit her ass all of a sudden. She was getting her clothes together one second, and within the next, that headache knocked her ass smooth the fuck out."

I was really laughing on the inside. She gone be pissed when she wakes up in the morning. I hit that bitch with that one and gone.

We pulled up to the club and gave them our names so we can be escorted to our VIP area. The club was thick, and usually I don't go out, but lately, I've just been trying to live because tomorrow isn't promised.

Stopping by the bar, I ordered a drink and sent two bottles to our table. Destiny was in her own zone with some cute guy all in her ear. I just fell back and sipped my drink. When the bottles came, I wasted no time turning it up.

"Slow down, sis," Destiny whispered in my ear.

"Girl, I'm good. I'm just trying to enjoy myself for once," I slurred.

"Ok, I'll keep my eyes on you. Take it easy, Summer." I gave her a fake smile like I was listening as I continued to pour up. It was starting to get hot as hell in the club, so I told her I was stepping outside.

Making my way slowly through the crowd, I felt myself getting sicker every step I took. I made it to the door, ran around the corner and started throwing up. A few minutes went by, I had finally stopped and got myself together. Turning back around, I stepped into a hole and twisted my ankle. I tried to stop myself from falling in the mud, but I couldn't. Suddenly, my body was pulled up right before I hit the ground.

"It's ok. I got you. I'll take care of you," he said just above a whisper.

"No, I'm good thanks."

Wiping myself off, I finally looked up, and all I saw was a black hoodie with a tiger head. I tried my best to scream, but my voice was caught in my throat. I couldn't see his face because he had the hood tied tight.

Feeling his hands wrap around my neck pulled my attention back to him, and my voice finally came.

"HEEELP! HEEEEELP! Please HEEELP MEE!"

"AYE LET HER GO!" I heard a voice yell out. He let my neck go and ran off in the opposite direction. I tried to catch my breath, as the guy came over to help me.

"Do you want me to call the police?" he asked, as he helped me out of the alley. Before I could reply, we bumped into Knight and Skillz.

"What the fuck are y'all doing?" he spat. Rushing to him, I threw my arms around his neck and started crying.

"He was here; he tried to kill me!" I sobbed.

"What? Who tried to kill you? Summer talk to me, baby. Who tried to kill you?"

"The guy in the dark," was all I said before I passed out in his arms.

※

Waking up in the bed with Knight beside me, I tried my best to pull myself up. My body was feeling like it had been hit by a freight train. I had the worst hangover ever and my fucking ankle was swollen. Rolling out of bed, I made my way to the bathroom the best way I could and started washing my face and brushing my teeth. My head was banging hard as hell, and for the first time ever, I could finally relate to Desire'. I'm sure I made her ass feel just like this.

Looking in the mirror, I noticed the handprints that were around my neck. I started to have a flashback of what happened last night. Dropping down to the floor, I pulled my knees to my chest, and I began to cry. Not just for me but for my sister as well. I can only imagine how scared she was when the guy did that shit to her.

I must have been sniffling too loud because Knight came into the bathroom to check on me. I was so glad the other guy stopped him, or I probably would be dead right now.

Sitting next to me, he pulled me into his broad shoulders.

"It's ok. I got you. I'll take care of you." the hairs stood up on my pussy when he said that.

"Something wasn't right about this. Why would the same person try to kill me too? I didn't even know what she was into. It was weird because it's like he knew where I was and that I was in that alley alone as if he had been watching me already. Even the other day when I was out, I started feeling like someone was watching and following me.

Shit, I thought it was you at first because we had just fallen out.

Every time I turned around no one was there. I just figured maybe I was just thinking too much about my sister and started hearing and seeing things." I was lost, broken and confused.

None of this shit is adding up, and I was kicking my own ass for not making Destiny come outside with me.

❧ 13 ☙

KNIGHT

I made sure my girl was good before I left out the house this morning. She had a rough ass night, and I was glad I was there to pick up the pieces. I just wished I was there to catch who it was because I would have taken his head off like I take doors off the hinges. We've only been dating a little while now, and all I want to do is protect her. If I could follow her daily, I would. Just to make sure everything is ok.

Coming up with an idea, I decided to swing by my brother's crib first. I have to go out of town for a few days, and this is the only person I can trust to keep an eye on her for me. I got out of the car right as his front door was opening up. Desire' stepped outside followed by TK who leaned in for a kiss.

"Hey, Knight. Bye Knight," she started as she walked down the steps.

"Damn bruh, when did that happen, and what the hell happened to her forehead?" The heffa had a big ass knot on her head.

"Man, me and Des', been fucking around for a minute now. As far as her forehead, she said she woke up like that. She came by to tell me she finally let Domano's ass go."

"Somebody played kickball with her shit." I was laughing hard as hell at her. "Shorty don't waste no time moving on, huh. We beat his ass at her bar-b-que yesterday." I chuckled because Desiré has always been a hoe, and my brother didn't take Snoop Dogs advice when he said, *we don't love them hoes.* His ass be falling for the okey-doke quick.

"Ahh, get off my girl," he scolded.

"Nigga, she's been your girl for a millisecond, shut the fuck up. She probably already in the car headed to see Domano. She ain't over that nigga that damn fast."

"Fuck you, bruh! Oh, somebody called looking for you today?"

"Who?"

"Dez nuts, ha!" he joked. "Now tell me what the fuck you want, I got shit to do for my girl."

I sucked my teeth first before I started to talk. "I'm going out of town with Skillz to see about opening up this club in Indiana. We will be gone for a day or two checking some places out. I want you to keep an eye on Summer for me. Just check in on her every so often."

"I got you, bruh. Just give me all of her info, and I'll make sure she's good."

"Good looking out. Oh, and don't wear that damn coat of yours either. That shit will scare the hell out of my girl."

"I don't have it anyway right now anyway, my girl took it."

"Which girl is this Des' or the coal that was here last week?"

"Fuck you mean coal?"

"The bitch was so black that she looked like a lump of coal sitting on the couch. Tar-baby, looking ass bitch."

"Maaan, you bogus as hell for that shit. She got some good pussy though. You know the blacker the berry, the sweeter the juice."

"That black bitch much be extra sweet then."

"You making jokes like you not dark, my nigga. Now get out, because I got shit to do." Dapping him up, I gave him Summer's information then left out his house. Satisfied, now I can go out of town in peace and not worry about if she is good or not. The very minute we close this deal, I'm headed straight to her.

"DON'T STOP, BABY I'M ABOUT TO CUM!" SUMMER moaned.

Her legs were wrapped around my shoulders as I got one last taste of her before we left. She rocked her hips on my tongue as I continued to hold her up in the palm of my hands. Feeling her juices cover my chin, I lifted her down to the bed and slid right inside of that juicy pussy. Holding her close to me, I dug deep inside of her. Her pussy had a tight grip on my dick like she didn't want to let go.

Slow stroking her, I licked and sucked on her right breast while caressing the left.

"This pussy feels so good," I mumbled.

BAM! BAM! BAM!

"Off yo ass and on yo feet, you don't have time to beat yo meat!" Skillz yelled, repeating the line off *Friday*. I wanted to laugh at that dummy, but I had to get this nut first.

"Booooy, if you don't get the fuck back," Summer hissed. Shaking my head, I leaned in and kissed her evil ass. Pulling me in deeper with her legs wrapped securely around my waist, she was making sure I didn't pull out. If I weren't crazy, I would think she was trying to get popped off.

She started grinding on my dick while I gave her deep strokes of death. Feeling my nut rising up like Andra Day song, I allowed it to coat the inside of her pussy. As my dick jerked inside of her, she started cumin' at the same time. I stayed inside the pussy a little bit longer just making sure I released everything before I pulled out.

Pulling out, I walked into the half bathroom and wet a towel for her. Coming back out, I started cleaning her off making sure her pussy was nice and clean until she made it home to shower. After I finished her, I went back in the bathroom and did the same to myself.

"You gone be straight while I'm gone?" I asked as we both got dressed.

"Yea, I'll be good, baby. Don't worry about me. I'm a big girl." I kissed her on the forehead.

"Promise to call me, for anything."

"I pinky promise, baby," she replied. I walked her to the door and laughed when she stuck her finger up at Skillz on her way out.

I locked up, we got in the car and headed to Indiana. The whole way there I prayed TK did what I asked. If not, I was fucking his ass up when I got back.

DESIRE'

Waking up in my closet the next morning, I was in a complete daze. My head was pounding, and I couldn't remember for the life of me what the fuck happened. I remembered getting my clothes ready, and that was it. I had a knot on my forehead the size of Texas, so I figured I hit my head and knocked myself out. I was even madder because them bitches didn't come and check on me, lay a bitch in the bed, or nothing Jesus.

When I woke up, Destiny was not home yet. I threw on some clothes, piled makeup on my forehead, and headed over to TK's house. He and I were fucking around a while ago before Domano and I started dating. When he would fuck up, I would slide my hot ass on TK's dick. He has always been a fool for me, and I could get his ass to do any damn thing. He drops more stacks on me than Domano ever has. Don't get me wrong, Dom broke bread too, but TK drops off racks. The only reason I never fully given myself to him was because his dick ain't no longer than a puppy penis, and ain't nobody got time for that.

KNOCK! KNOCK!

I was standing at the door impatiently waiting for TK to open up.

"You couldn't call first?" he spat, as soon as the door swung open.

"Do I ever? Now, unless you got a bitch in here, then I didn't have to call first. Now get over here and eat this pussy to make my damn head stop hurting."

Doing as he was told with no questions asked he licked those sexy full lips of his and rubbed his hands together. Removing my leggings, I revealed my freshly waxed pussy. He dropped down to his knees and threw my legs over his shoulders. Putting his hands firmly on my back, he held me in place while he started slowly licking up and down my slit. Making his way to my clit, he gently sucked on it, making my body quiver.

"Hmm TK, right there." I pushed his head deeper in between my thighs as I grind slowly on his tongue.

"This pussy taste so fucking good, Des', fuck!"

"I knoow shit, tell me what it tastes like." He started eating me like he was really trying to get a good taste of it.

"Dressing."

"Dressing?" I replied quickly.

"Yea, ma." Throwing my legs back, he was now paying close atten-tion to my ass. "Dressing, yams, and greens, with sweet potato pie on the side." This nigga must have lost his damn mind. I pushed his head back out of the way.

"Move," I hissed, frustrated as hell at him. Who the fuck tell someone their pussy taste like a full course Thanksgiving dinner?

"BITCH, SHUT THE FUCK UP! I AIN'T DONE WITH YOU YET." Looking at him in shock, my pussy started dripping immedi-ately. I have never been so turned on in my life. He has never talked to me like this before. It was like the nigga done grew an extra nine inches on his dick or something.

Snatching me up off the couch, he kissed me roughly as he carried me down the hall into his bedroom.

"I'm about to tear this pussy up, girl," he lied... I mean he stated as he got undressed.

He laid me back on the bed and started tickling my pussy with his finger. It was feeling good, but I was ready for him to put it in. I started grinding against his finger, trying to let him know I wanted the dick now without saying it.

"You like that shit, don't you? I told you I was gonna tear this pussy up, girl."

"Hmm yes daddy, now put it in already!" I requested, feeling myself getting anxious. I wasn't going to feel the pressure that I get from Domano, but that little dick be tickling my pussy enough to make me cum.

"It is in, Des'." Looking at him, and then looking down at his hands, they were both on my body already. It was his dick the entire time.

"OH YES DADDY, RIGHT THERE! HARDER TK, HARDER!" Y'all should have seen the way his smile grew big when I said that.

"I'M ABOUT TO CUM. I'M ABOUT TO CUM. OOOOOOH SHIIIIIT!" I lied.

"Yeaaa, daddy got that dope dick," he stated, trying to pump himself up. Getting this shit over with, I did a quick jiggle on his dick, and he started cumin' faster than a broke bitch getting dress for free before eleven at the club.

"Damn girl, you woe a nigga out."

"I'll see you tonight, right?"

"You know I got you, ma."

After getting dressed he walked me outside, kissing me on the forehead. I turned away, only to see Knight walking up the stairs. I walked passed him quickly trying to hide the mysterious knot on my forehead.

"Hey, Knight... Bye Knight."

✂ 14 ✂

SUMMER

Knight is gone out of town, so my ass has been sitting around the house looking dumb. Going over my checklist for graduation, I was making sure I have all of my shit together. I can't believe that I will be graduating with my Bachelors in Elementary Education in just three weeks. My life has been such a mess since Sunny died and until the other day, I thought things were finally getting back on track.

I still cannot figure out for the life of me what the hell is going on. Just knowing someone is either following me or being told my whereabouts scares the shit out of me. I told Knight that I would be good only because my ass doesn't plan on coming outside. So until his fine ass comes home. I'm in.

Oh, Destiny called me this morning and asked if I knew what happened to Desire'. She said she woke up with a big ass knot on her head, and she doesn't know how. I laughed hard as fuck on the inside but replied with concern on the outside. I hit her ass hard, but I bet it still ain't knock sense into her ass. All she does is throw shots at my sister, and it's been like this before she got killed. I remember this one time they went toe to toe and Sunny was tearing that ass up.

"You want to go over Destiny and Des' house with me?" I asked Sunny.

Unlike most days, today is actually a good day for her. She's been upbeat and in a good mood all morning. I knew something was up, but I just couldn't put my finger on it. Usually, it will take her a couple of hours after she wakes up to get out of the groggy mood she was in. Not today though, today she was acting like she got some good dick last night or something.

Oh my, that's what it is.

"Nah, I'm cool. I just want to sit here and bask in the glory of getting this cherry popped last night," she squealed.

"I knew it. Bitch, spill it I want the details asap, sis."

Sunny was a late bloomer. Although I had lost my virginity in high school to Alex, she still was holding on to hers. Our parents scared the shit out of us to making us not want to have sex until we were married. Once I got my first taste of an orgasm, it was over with. Alex and I fucked like jackrabbits until he went away to school. After that, it took me a few years before I had sex with anyone else. Matter of fact, it's going on year two now, and I'm perfectly fine with being dick deprived. We are 21 now, so it was about time she gave that V-card to a valuable person.

"Didn't mama say, a lady never kisses and tells?"

"Yea, but I'm pretty sure she only meant that if we did something that we had no business doing. Then we need to keep that shit to ourselves, but this right here is juicy, and I wanna know with who, where, for how long, did it hurt, was it good, and is he fine?" Spitting out question after question, she gave me the damn bitch face.

"Really twin?" she questioned.

"You lucky I didn't ask how big it was... now give me the tea."

"Uuugh, you aggy as fuck, twin. Anyway, his name is Domano Dora. Where we do it at?"

"Hol' up!" I yelled, stopping her from saying any more. "Who was it?"

"Domano."

"Twwwwin, you didn't! You do know that's Desire' man, right?"

"Umm, he told me they were not together and something about her pussy not having power. Whatever the hell that means."

I had to laugh on the inside at that part. I hate that she is so gullible and will fall for shit like this. The fact that I just saw Domano with Des' yesterday morning proves that he a lying, dirty dick nigga.

"Get dressed," I announced.

Getting up from the bed we were just sitting on, I started to get dressed and so did she. We walked the few blocks down to Desire' and Destiny's apartment and let ourselves in. We all had a key to each other's place in case of emergency, and in my eyes, this is one. When your boyfriend cheats with your best friend, that's most definitely something that needs to be told right now.

"DESIIIRE'!" I yelled out to her.

"WHAAAT? WHO DIED? WHAT'S GOING ON?" she exclaimed, rushing out of the room.

"No one died, girl."

"Why are you calling my damn name like that then?" she questioned.

"Sunny has something to tell you."

"No, I don't," Sunny replied nonchalantly.

"Ugh, yea you do. We've talked about this before we came over here."

"Ugh, no you did. I didn't agree to this shit. You felt she needed to know, so I feel you need to tell her. If it's up to me, she ain't gotta know nothing. They're not together anymore sooo..." Sunny was not getting it at all. As a friend, this is what you supposed to do. It wasn't just on Domano that they fuck, it was on her too.

"Somebody needs to speak because I have somewhere to be," Des' interrupted.

"Look, Des'. Yesterday I fucked Domano. He finessed me out of my panties before I had a chance to tell his ass I was a virgin. We fucked at his place, it hurt like hell, his dick was big, and yes I will do it again."

Standing there with my mouth open wide as fuck, I didn't expect her to say all that.

"You happy now, Summer?"

"YOU NASTY, CRAZY BITCH!"

I don't know what she said that for. Sunny hate when people call her crazy, especially if she's having a good day. She and Desire' started fighting like pit bulls. I tried to break them up, but that shit wasn't happening. Des' started getting the best of Sunny, and then it was like something clicked. Sunny eyes went black, and that bitch was out for blood. We couldn't get her to stop, so I had to call daddy to come down and help.

"SUNNY STOP!!" was all he said, and she instantly stopped beating her ass and started shaking.

"I got something for you, bitch," Desire' whispered as she tried to lift her head, but it quickly fell back down.

After everything happened, I kinda regretted making her tell what happened, but shit, Des' deserved that ass whooping. She never stopped fucking with Domano, so apparently, she didn't give a fuck, or he fed her some good bullshit.

Hearing my phone ring, I looked at the screen and noticed it was Knight calling.

"Heyyy daddy, I miss you," I said as soon as I answered.

"I miss yo pretty ass too. What are you doing?"

"Nothing, lying around the house bored as hell."

"Get out the house and go find a dress for your graduation or something. I will send TK by to check on you later on."

"Ugh, I guess. I will call you and let you know where I am going."

"Ok, be safe. I'll be home later tonight."

Ending the call with him, I jumped in the shower so that I could get this day started. Getting out, I threw on one of my PINK outfits and some Huaraches and headed out the door. I decided to look around in North Riverside Mall to see what they have. Walking around going from store to store, I finally stopped in Forever 21. They usually have some cute dresses, and I won't be in the shit long anyway, so anything black, tight and cute will do for me.

Finding the perfect dress, I bought it and headed to ALDO to find some shoes. I know I have plenty at home, but nothing is wrong with adding more to your collection. I found this cute pair of black heels that went perfectly with my dress. Satisfied with this not taking forever, I left out the mall to grab me something to eat.

I texted Knight to tell him what I found and that I was headed to get a beef from Nick's then back home. I was over this day already, and it just started. Getting out the car, I headed into the restaurant to order my food.

Feeling someone blow hard in my ear caused me to jump.

"What the fuck?" I spat.

"What's good, sis?" Turning around quickly, seeing TK standing right behind me. That was the weirdest shit ever, and I had to make a note of that to tell Knight.

"Yo ass almost got fucked up. Don't be blowing in my damn ear like that."

"My bad, sis. I had to get your attention some kind of way."

"How about addressing me by my name," I hissed irritated as fuck. I grabbed my food and headed out the door.

"Summer, I'm sorry to hear about your twin sister. Knight told me that she got killed and the dude had on one of my hoodies. I wish I could help and tell you who it was, but it was so many people who bought that shit."

"Yea it's cool. Anyway, I have to get home."

"That's cool. You be safe. These streets are vicious at night time. So make sure you lock up." Giving him a fake smile, I slammed my car door and headed home. *What the fuck is wrong with that nigga?* I said to myself.

Pulling up at home, I did exactly what he said when I got inside. I made sure everything was locked and started eating my food. It was seven o'clock at night, and I was ready to lay it down. Pouring me a glass of wine, I grabbed my iPad and got in bed. Finding this book called *You Should Be My Shawty* by Manda P. I needed something to take me into another world until I drifted off to sleep.

BEEP!

Picking up the phone, I saw it was a text from Knight, so I quickly opened it.

Hinge Breaker: I will be home in 30 minutes so have the door unlocked and the pussy ready for me.

Me: You silly, but I sure will. HURRY UP!!

Tossing my phone on the bed, I put my iPad up and started moving around the room to get ready. I'm in need of some good dick too, so I need to have this pussy nice and wet when he walked in the house. I jumped back in the shower making sure I was extra clean and started walking around my room to let myself air dry before I put my lotion on. I also lit candles and turned on music to set the mood. The weather was nice out, so I let my window up that's right next to my bed to let a nice breeze in.

Putting my phone on Chris Brown's "Covered in You", I started putting my lotion on and got into the bed. I laid in bed and started rubbing myself slowly, easing my hand down my body until I reached my inner thighs. Rubbing my hand over the top of my pussy, I opened my lips up. Using my other hand, I inserted two fingers into my pussy. I started playing in my wetness and rubbing my clit at the same time. Closing my eyes, I kept rubbing my clit and used my now free hand to rub and squeeze on my breasts as my hips slow grind against my hand.

Remembering I forgot to unlock the door but I was too caught up in this feeling to get up. Hopefully he remembers where I put the spare key, cause I ain't getting up.

"Shiiit!" I moaned out. Hearing the front door open made me get even more excited. "Hmm, daddy! It's about ti..." I moaned, but my sentence was cut short by a hand covering up my mouth aggressively.

Opening my eyes, all I saw was a tiger face, and my heart started racing. I tried my best to get up and away, but I couldn't. Feeling my legs being forced open, he rammed his dick inside of me, and it hurt so badly that I winced in pain.

Biting his hand, trying to do all I could to make him stop.

BAM! He hit me so hard that it dazed me. Shaking the dizziness off, he grabbed both of my hands with one hand as he continued to force himself inside of me.

"PLEASE STOP!!" I screamed out.

"SUMMER!" I heard Knight yell out. When he heard Knight rushing down the hall, he pulled out of me and jumped out the window. Frantically jumping up, I ran right into Knight's arms. "BABY, WHAT'S WRONG?" he asked.

"HE WAS HERE!" I screamed, pointing towards the window.

I dropped down to my knees as Knight ran outside to see if he could see anyone. Crying hysterically, my heart was still racing. Knight came back in and started helping me put my clothes on.

"We gotta get you dressed and to the hospital," I nodded my head ok and started moving around slowly.

KNIGHT

Summer front door was open wide when I got out the car, so I rushed up the stairs with my gun drawn. Hearing her scream out *PLEASE STOP* made my heart start racing. That's all I kept hearing in my head as I rushed her to the hospital. Once we made it inside, I lifted her out of the car and ran inside of the ER.

"HELP! MY GIRL WAS JUST ATTACKED!" Some nurses ran over and grabbed her out of my arms and placed her in a wheelchair. Taking her to the back, I tried my best to get back there with her, but they wouldn't allow me too.

Pulling my phone out, I called up her brother Marquise and told him what happened. I started pacing the floor back and forth with so much going through my head. I was kicking my own ass because I shouldn't have left her alone after the other night and most definitely shouldn't have told her to leave her door open for me.

"FUCK!" I yelled out as I punched the wall that was in front of me.

I waited up front until Marquise and her mom came running inside. They then allowed all of us to the back with her.

"Oh my baby, are you ok?" her mom cried out as she saw Summer lying in bed in the fetal position. She had tears pouring out of her eyes, and it was a bruise on her right cheek.

The door opened up, and the doctor walked in with a lady detective behind her.

"Hello Miss Daze, how are you feeling?" she asked Summer.

"I'm ok," she replied while sobbing.

"We perform a rape kit on your daughter, and we found fibers of silicon and another woman's bodily fluids inside of you." Everyone quickly turned their head to her in confusion.

"What do you mean another woman? I was just raped, and I felt his nasty ass dick inside of me!"

"Yes Summer I understand that but..."

"You mean to tell me he did this to another bitch before he did it to me?" Summer asked not giving the doctor a chance to speak.

"Summer, what I'm saying is, a man may or may not have raped you, sweetheart. The fibers of silicon that we found were more than likely from a dildo."

"WHAT THE FUCK?" we all said in unison.

"I'm not understanding this shit at all. Who would do something so fucking disgusting like this?"

"Unfortunately, we were unable to find out who the other fluids were from. She's not in our database, but I promise you we will find out what happened to you," the detective stated to Summer."

"Just like you guys did for my sister. Just please leave. You guys aren't going to do shit but act like you care, fake like you are out looking, but really be sitting behind your desk and popping donut holes in your mouth all day."

"I understand your frustration and..."

"ARE YOU DEAF OR JUST DUMB? I SAID GET THE FUCK OUT!" the detective looked at Summer and then moved away from the bed.

"I will keep in touch," she said to Mrs. Daze as she passed her a business card.

"We will be discharging you in a few, and if you think of anything in specific that we need to know, then please come back in or go to the police."

The doctor left out of the room, and it fell into an awkward silence until Summer finally spoke up.

"Did you set me up?" I started looking around the room to see who the hell she was talking to. "You, Knight. Did you or did you not set me up to get raped or whatever the fuck you call it since it wasn't a real dick?"

"What? Why the fuck would I do some shit like that? I brought yo ass right here, so if I did this shit, I wouldn't have given two fucks about you getting to the hospital."

"That was just a cover-up. So, tell me who was the bitch, nigga, or whatever! Y'all mother fuckers got my head so fucked up that I don't know what's going on. Either y'all setting me up to get killed or to go the fuck to an insane asylum cause the insane part is most definitely working."

"Are you listening to yourself right now?" I questioned.

"Why would your brother magically bump into me after I told you where I was at getting food? Huh? Or why would he bring up me having a twin sister and her getting killed? Oooh and not just that, but the little weird mother fucker blew in my ear like he was blowing a gah damn dandelion."

"Wait what? When did this happen?"

"It's doesn't matter just get out! Don't come around me again cause ever since you came into my life nothing but weird shit has been happening."

"Summer, just listen..."

"Don't walk up on her like that, bruh!" Marquise intervened. I looked him up and down, I started to knock his ass green eyed ass out.

"Aight, you got it. Do you, ma!" I stated as I turned to leave the hospital. Summer was talking out the side of her neck, and I ain't have time to keep going back and forth over this shit.

15

SUMMER

I was released from the hospital a few days ago, and instead of going home, I went to my mama's house. I refuse to go back home right now. That place is giving me nothing but bad memories— bad memories about my sister, Knight, and last but not least about the nasty ass mother fucker who raped me with a dirty ass dildo. That was the sickest shit I've ever heard of. I made them test me for everything under the sun because I'll be damn if I take a bath and my coochie floats off.

"Hey baby girl, how are you feeling?" my mama asked, walking in the bedroom carrying a basket of clothes.

"I'm good, ma just sitting here looking crazy. I don't feel like getting up to go to this darn school."

"I'm going to the grocery store a little later. Do you wanna go with me and pick out some of the things you want to eat since it looks like you're not leaving anytime soon."

"I sholl ain't leaving and nah I don't wanna go because you gone end up at Target buying something you don't need."

"Girl, whatever!" She waved me off. "Have you heard from Trench? You know that boy didn't do this to you, right?" I rolled my eyes because I really didn't want to talk about him now or later.

"No, and I'm not trying to either. Like I said at the hospital, it's not adding up, and I'm not taking any chances with him or his brother."

"Baby, I could tell by the way that man was pacing when we walked in the hospital that he was worried about you. Marquise was here when he called, and I could hear it all in his voice. I don't know what this other shit is, but he has nothing to do with it. Forgive that man before you lose that man."

"I'll think about it. Let me get up so that I can go pay the last of these fees."

"Oh, I have the sexiest dress to wear to your graduation. Your father said after 23 years, I've finally snapped back." She stood up and did her little spin.

I laughed because her and my father swear they are still young. My mother works out every other day, and her body is amazing. I hope I look half as good as she does when I get older. She left out the room, and I started finding clothes to put on. Graduation is less than two weeks away, and I have to pay the last of my tuition and graduation fees. Student loans are raked up, and Sally Mae is gone have to wait until I find a job before she gets a penny from my ass.

Finding a pair of light distressed skinny jeans and a hunter green bodysuit top, I paired them with some cute hunter green flats that I bought from Old Navy. Grabbing my Chloe' bag that I took back from Desire', I then headed out the door. The weather was nice today. We were in the mid-70s, and for us Midwest people, that's nice as hell.

Jumping on the expressway, I cruised all the way to CSU. My music was blaring, and for the first time my mind was free of all the bullshit, and I was at peace, for the moment.

Arriving, I found a parking spot and headed to the financial aid office. At first, I was beyond pissed about the things Sunny was doing, but I can't even lie like that money she left behind didn't come in handy. I had more than enough to pay my fees for graduation and the last payment of my tuition.

"Good afternoon, Mrs. Dolce'."

"Hey, sweetie, I'm glad you came by. I was just about to mail these receipts off to you."

"Receipts for what?"

"Your fees, Summer. Everything is paid in full, including all of your student loans. So here are the receipts for your tuition, graduation, and your loans you took out over the years."

I was standing there looking crazy as hell. I wish my mom would have told me she paid everything for me before I got out of bed this morning. Maybe she just wanted to surprise me or something.

"I didn't know everything was paid, Mrs. Dolce'. I'm actually here to pay it myself."

"Well, now you can save that money because Mr. Knight took care of everything for you. Not only is he generous, he's also handsome." She winked at me.

"Yea he can be nice when he wanna be. Thank you, Mrs. Dolce'. Oh, if you don't mind me asking when did he pay all of this?"

"Just a few days ago, Mr. Knight came in and told me that he had to take you to the emergency room. You weren't feeling well and that he wanted to do something nice for you."

Smiling at her before turning to walk away, I replied, "Thanks."

Heading back to my car, I jumped in and did the dash all the way to Knight's place.

Pulling up, I got out the car and made sure I grabbed the bag of money.

BAM! BAM! BAM!

BAM! BAM! BAM!

I knocked on the door until it came flying open. He stood there with a mean mug, no shirt, some basketball shorts, and a print that made me lose my train of thought.

"WHAT!" he shouted.

"DON'T FUCKING WHAT ME. I just came over here to give you your money back. No one asked you for help and as far as I'm concerned this is just your way of apologizing for the bullshit you pulled."

"Summer, either take yo ass home with all of this bullshit or come in here and talk to me like you got some fucking sense."

"Why did you do it? You think this shit supposed to make me forget everything and fall for you all over again. Well, it's not gonna happen!" I exclaimed. The more I yelled out of frustration, the closer

I walked up on him so that he could know he didn't intimidate me at all.

"You might as well stop all of those chec…"

Before I finished my sentence, he had pressed his soft, sexy, full lips against mine. Lifting me up off the ground, he kissed me and closed the door behind us.

"You gone learn to calm the fuck down when I tell you to," he whispered in between kisses. "I did that shit because I love you girl, not for an apology that I don't owe yo ass. Ever since I met you, I wanted to make you happy, to protect you, and to love you for life. Regardless of what you said in the hospital, that shit didn't stop anything. You were confused and hurt, and I understood that, and that's why I left." The more he looked into my eyes and spoke to me, the more I could tell he was telling the truth.

We were now standing in his living room with me still wrapped around his waist.

"As your man, I couldn't allow you to struggle and pay all of that shit off, especially since I had the money. You worked hard to finish school, and I wanted to take away one less thing for you to worry about. Now you take that money and do what you want with it. Don't fight me on this because I'm not stopping not one check."

As I started to speak again, he cut me off with a more deep and passionate kiss. This time it resulted in these tight ass jeans coming off and my pussy sliding down his dick.

KNIGHT

I wanted to do something special for Summer since she was having a rough time, even after her ass flipped out on me at the hospital. I knew the shit wasn't true, so I still did what her man was supposed to do for her— make shit easier. Had I known she was going to react the way she did, would I have still done it? FUCK YEA, especially if it would have her pretty ass on my dick right now. Plus, makeup sex is the best sex.

"Throw that shit back, ma!" Smacking her on the ass, I watched as it jiggled like a big breasted bitch walking around with no bra.

She started throwing it back and gripping my dick like she was snatching my nut out. That shit was feeling so good that I had to pull out and eat her pussy. She wasn't about make me nut in a couple of minutes. Flipping her over on her side, I put one leg in the air as I watched my dick slide in and out of her juices. My baby pussy is so pretty, and now that those cuts finally healed after she shaved before going on stage, it's extra pretty now.

"Baby, oooh shit, I'm about to cum."

Sliding out, I went down and started sucking on her clit. She went bananas as I sucked her nut out. As soon as I saw her coming down off her orgasmic high, I slid my dick back in and went to work, making sure I didn't let up until my nut was shooting out like an Uzi. Lying down beside her, I wrapped my arm around her waist and kissed her softly on her neck.

"I love you, Summer Reign."

"I love you more, Trench Michael Knox Knight."

"Really?" I asked making her giggled.

It's crazy how we have only been dating for a little while but have been through more shit than a little bit. Honestly, I wouldn't change shit about it. I plan on taking her on another trip after her graduation. It's still some things we need to learn about each other and what better way to do it other than relaxing on the beach with clear blue water, splashing on her sexy ass body.

"Knight?"

"Yea."

"I'm late."

"Get yo ass up and go where you need to be. I'll be here when you get back waiting to blow that pussy cap back blue," I joked.

"Boy, I don't have anywhere to go. I'm talking about my cycle; I'm a week late."

"Get yo ass up and go to the store and get what you need then. Wait... who's is it? You did let a dildo raw dog you." She hit me in the head so fast and hard.

"Oh, I see yo ass got jokes. How bout I just take my ass to the chopping block, so I won't have to worry about if you are the father or not."

Rolling on top of her playfully, I pinned her down to the bed.

"Don't play with me like that. You ain't gone do nothing to my shorty but bring him here healthy so that he can get spoiled. Now get up so we can get a test."

"I have one in my purse."

"And you still lying in bed? Go piss on the shit and see what's up."

She got up, went to her purse, and sashayed to the bathroom. She must be full of baby because she pissed and came out less than a minute with a positive test. Judging by the look on her face, she wasn't all that excited but shit, my dick was jumping for joy. I ain't ever had no pregnant pussy before, so I'm trying to see what that be like.

"Why are you looking like that, Summer?"

"I'm not ready to be a mother, and my biggest fear is that my child will be like my sister or my grandmother. Both of them were schizophrenic, and I don't want my child to suffer like that."

"You can't go into this thinking negatively. What if it wasn't your sister, but it was you? Would you want someone to base their life decisions off a condition that you have, a condition that you had no control over at that? This baby that's growing in you is a blessing, and I do know that God will never put more on us than we can handle.

You have me, your parents, your brothers, and my mom all behind you with this. You're going to be the best mother ever." Kissing her on the forehead, I hoped that I ease her mind just a little bit.

Most men my age aren't ready to settle down, but I am. I've lived that wild life before selling drugs and killing people for disrespecting me or not having my money. That shit took eight years of my life from me, and ain't nothing worth my freedom anymore. I want this baby more than anything. Why she thinks I've been bussing in her every chance I got.

"Let's go eat. A nigga can only eat pussy for so long before he needs some real food in his stomach."

"Oooh only if we are going to Chipotle's." Grabbing our things, we then headed out the door.

❦ 16 ❦

MARQUISE

I let MJ stay at my mom crib last night because I had some shit to do at the club today. Matter of fact, I'm almost late for the meeting now. Skillz ass be on some 'if you on time you're late, bullshit' like we in the fucking military. I don't see how many meeting we gotta have about running a strip club. You get the bitches, pack the club out with thirsty niggas, and make sure the hoes clean. You know in case they wanna dibble and dabble in some other shit.

Fuck, let me get my shit together before a nigga be late as fuck for real. Pulling my boxers out the dresser, I tossed them on the bed and jumped in the shower, making sure I washed off the juices of this lil shorty I fucked with last night. She was one of the dancers at the club and shorty had been begging to give me the pussy ever since she started working there.

I was trying to be a good dude to Meka, so I didn't fuck her the first time she asked. I waited until the second time. I had to show myself I had some true willpower to be faithful and shit. I think I did a damn good job.

Getting out the shower, I dried off and started getting dressed. I'm a simple nigga, so a Nike sweat suit was good for me. Sliding my boxers and my sweats on, I started walking around the room looking for my

Movado watch. I was gone be .38 hot if that lil bitch stole my shit on her way out.

"WHAT THE FUCK!" I yelled out once I felt my dick burning and itching all at once.

Stepping out of my clothes quickly, I started checking my dick to see what the fuck was wrong. It literally feels like someone was setting fire to my dick, and it was itching worse than a bitch head when she kept her weave in too long.

"THE FUCK IS WRONG WITH MY DICK?" I questioned myself as I jumped back in the damn shower trying to cool my dick off and stop the itching.

A nigga was scratching like he had rabies or some shit. I'm worried about the bitch stealing my watch, but it looks like the bitch done gave me an instant STD. Getting out the shower, I rushed into the kitchen to grab me a bag of peas out the freezer to cool my dick off. I'm a red nigga, so you see all of the scratch marks and bumps from the instant STD the bitch gave my ass. I couldn't wait to get to the club so that I could fire that nasty bitch and have Summer beat her ass.

"Payback is a bitch, huh?" I turned around with the bag of peas on my dick only to see Tameka uglass sitting in my living room.

"Bitch, what the fuck did you do to my dick, and how the fuck did you get in my shit?"

"You lucky it was just icy hot and itch powder in yo draws. I started to Google a way to melt down hot Takis and shoot the liquid up the tip of your dick in a syringe. Oh and as far as how I got in... you never got your keys back."

"BITCH!" I blurted out, as I chucked the bag of peas at her head hard as I could. Pulling my gun from the countertop, I walked over and put it to her head. "Get yo ass up and come clean this shit off me."

"Marquise, you started this shit. I'm not about to do shit. Couldn't nobody help me get those fucking hot ass chips out my asshole. I had to wait until them bitches dissolved then they came running out like water!" she yelled out, walking to my bedroom.

"Yep, I started it, and I'm gone finish this shit too. Now come suck my dick until this shit stop burning."

"But it's gone burn my mouth, Quise," she stated with her head cocked to the side trying to force tears out.

"Who gives a fuck, now suck this dick."

Dropping down to her knees, she grabbed some lotion and started massaging all around my dick as she sucked on the head. The more she rubbed and sucked, the better that shit started feeling. This bitch had the game fucked up if she thought she was about to icy hot a nigga and leave. She's gone suck this dick until her lips numb.

⁙

"It's about time yo ass decided to show up," Skillz hissed as I walked in the office.

"Yea, I had a heated situation I had to deal with before I came."

"Yea, I hear you. Anyway, let's get this shit over with. It's me and my wife's anniversary, and she wants to go to New Orleans for the weekend."

"So, what's up?" Knight asked. I looked at this nigga, and he looked anxious to get out this bitch too. I haven't seen him since Summer made him leave the hospital. I made a mental note to talk to his ass once this was over.

"What happened to your sister? She was one of the best dancers out there, and after a few weeks, she just disappeared. I thought the fool that threw the tomato at her scared her ass off or something."

"Bruh, Sunny got killed over a month ago. That wasn't even her a few weeks ago up there, was her Summer."

"What the hell? Why didn't you tell me?"

"Because I don't like mother fuckers acting like they care and giving me their weak ass condolences. When she got killed, my mother didn't want to broadcast the shit, so she's been talking to the detectives on the low trying to figure this shit out though.

It's a long ass story. Honestly, we don't know who did the shit. Summer's ass has been trying to play detective, but that shit is only gone end up getting her ass hurt."

"Nah, I got her... she's good." Knight interrupted. "She ain't playing detective no more; she is gone let the police do their job and leave it at that." Sucking my teeth, I looked at him intensely.

"Well, I'm sorry to hear that and if y'all need anything then, just let us know and that's real shit. Tell Summer to stay her ass out of the club. She's round here tricking mother fuckers," he joked. "Anyway, I just wanted to give y'all the profit we brought in for the past month. Business has been good.

Oh and we got the approval for the club in Indiana, and I'm looking to have that up and running by spring. Of course, I'ma need someone to run it, sooo if either one of you is looking to relocate, just let me know."

I looked at that nigga like he shitted in my cereal. He knows damn well I ain't moving to no damn Indiana. He can kick rocks with that shit.

"Yea aight, if that's all. I need to go pick up my little boy."

"Go head," Skillz replied as he started gathering up his things to leave.

"Aye Knight, can I holla at you for a minute?" I asked as we walked out of the office.

I needed to see where his head was at with my sister. Summer is a private person, and she doesn't like to tell my ass shit. She thinks I overreact to everything, but to me, I'm just being a big brother and making sure she's good.

KNIGHT

I really wasn't in the mood for all the extra shit today. I was gone get this meeting over with and go back to my girl, but it seems like Marquise has other plans.

"Sup bruh, what's good?" I asked as we stepped outside.

"Shit, just checking in on you and sis. How's that going?"

"We're good. We just found out we are expecting a shorty."

"She's expecting." he started, correcting me.

"Nah, I said it right. We are expecting. She's not going through none of this alone. That's my shorty and I'ma be there every step of the way. I'm in this shit for the long haul. Every doctor's appointment and every emotional break down her ass has, I'ma be there to let her know I got her. So, you don't have to worry about lil sis anymore because I got her. You just worry about why you stuck those Takis up shorty's ass," I joked.

"Bruh, how did you find out about that?"

"Tameka got a big ass mouth. She wasted no time telling mother fuckers how dirty you are, and what you did to her. That shit was funny as fuck. You gotta be a crazy mother fucker to think of some shit like that, for real."

"It was the only hole I could work with without her seeing me do the shit. Hey, it was either that or her pussy. She really was gone be around here burning." He started laughing hard as hell, and I can't even lie like I hesitated to join in.

"On some serious shit, you do right by my sister though. I'd hate to kill yo ass."

Usually, I wouldn't have taken offense to that shit, but I get it. If I had a little sister, I would be the same way. He ain't gotta worry about me though because I ain't checking for no shorties but my own.

We chopped it up for a little bit longer until I got a text from Summer asking me to bring her some Popeye's home.

"I gotta go, Summer is hungry."

"Tell her don't start that shit already. She's a half a day pregnant and all of a sudden got cravings and eating up everything. I wish you the best with her lil spoiled ass."

"Yea, I think I'ma need to be lifted up in prayer already." We laughed and headed to our cars. Jumping on the e-way, I did the dash to pick up her food.

Pulling back up in front of my place, I walked in only to find my mama and Summer sitting at the kitchen table. Summer was sitting there while mama placed all types of food in front of her so she could eat. That's one thing about mama; her ass is gone make sure you eat.

"UH UUMM!" I cleared my throat to get their attention. "I got your Popeyes but looks like I can eat this since mama got you covered."

"Why didn't you bring this beautiful soul by the house for me to meet her? I came over here to clean up for you and bring you leftovers. She's sitting in the bed staring at a pregnancy test as if it was gonna turn negative."

WHAP!

She hit my ass over the head with her towel that was thrown over her shoulder.

"And why you ain't tell me you round here fucking people with no protection. I told you about them trap thirst girls."

"Ma, if you don't get. I ain't gotta tell you nothing first off, and Summer isn't like those thirst trap girls who are only looking for a come up."

"I know she ain't because I know her mother and father. They had these girls so spoiled when they were younger that they had no reason to trap a nigga."

"I didn't know you knew her parents."

"Yeaaa baby, we all hung out back in the day. You know, before your father used to beat me black and blue daily. I stopped coming outside then because my face and body would be so fucked up. Stacy, Summer's mother, she didn't play that shit.

Once she saw the first bruise, she was ready to tear some shit up. Matter of fact, one time she did, and it took your father, me, and a crack head to get her off his ass. This is before you were born; I only had your older brother at the time. They moved away to the suburbs, and I was stuck to fight my battles on my own."

"Why didn't you ever leave him?" Summer asked.

This is a question I have been trying to get answered for years before it even came to the point of him getting killed. That would have prevented a lot of shit. Instead, she stayed and kept having fucking babies, even after he beat a few of the babies out of her. That still wasn't enough to get her to leave.

"You know, baby. I asked myself that over and over again. That man had broken me down so low that I thought no other man would even look at me. He made me thinking I was the problem. He kept saying if I left him I would only take those same problems to a new man, that new man would only beat my ass too. He had my head so fucked up, and I regret not taking my boys and moving far away from Chicago.

The more babies I had, the harder it was for me to find a job. I had to be home by a certain time to cook before the boys came home from school, make sure the house was clean, and his clothes were clean for work. It's hard to move far away with no money. He made sure he kept my pockets filled with the bare minimum— nothing more, nothing less."

"I'm sorry you had to go through that. I'm not trying to be funny or anything, so please don't take this the wrong way. But, is that hereditary? You know that beating up your woman stuff." My mom looked at Summer like she had three heads before she burst into laughter.

"No baby. That shit doesn't run through your blood. That's some dumb shit you pick up as a child, or hell even as an adult. His father did it to his mother. Therefore their father thought that's how you get your woman to listen. If you're asking if Knight is like that, the answer is no.

Now, if you were with Turk, the answered would have been, bitch yes. Get out now, pass go and please don't collect the 200 dollars to get out of jail because that's the safest place for you." She chuckled.

"He couldn't have been that bad." Ma and I both looked at her sideways.

"Does a bear shit in the woods and wipe his ass with a white bunny? Hell yea, he was that bad!"

My mama be saying some crazy shit sometimes for real, but I love my OG. We all sat around the table eating all the food she brought over. She and Summer continued to talk to get to know each other more. I was taking it all in because of course Summer and I are still getting to know each other too. Shit moved fast but oh well, I'm happy with how things are going, so I'm not complaining one bit.

17

SUMMER

I haven't seen Destiny or Desire in a while, so I decided to go by there to see if they wanted to have lunch with me. I haven't filled them in on everything that has been happening to me over the past week. After a dildo raped me, I closed everyone off for a few days.

I stayed at my mom's, and ever since I found out I was pregnant, Knight has made me practically move in with him. He has been waiting on me hand and foot. I can't lie like I haven't been enjoying that shit either.

I like him being close to me at night because the events of that night still play in my head. Here I am lying in bed thinking I'm about to get the business by my man, only for a nasty fucker to beat him to it. I was mad because that lil plastic thing hit my damn spot and it took everything in me to hold that nut in. I was not about to even give him the satisfaction of making me cum that damn fast or cum period at a time like that.

KNOCK! KNOCK!

"Hey boo," Destiny greeted.

"Hey, love. I came by to see if you guys wanted to go out to lunch. It's nice out, and I have sooo much to talk about."

"I'm always down to eat; you know that. Desire', on the other hand, might not be up to it, but you can ask her."

Walking down the hall to Desire's room, I started laughing to myself thinking about the look she had on her face when I knocked her ass out that night. She went stumbling back into that closet and hit her head on the dresser that was in her closet.

Why she got a dresser in the closet, I don't know, but I bet she wishes she didn't. She probably would have been ok after I punched her, but that damn dresser did not spare her at all. It knocked that ass clean the fuck out.

"Hey Des, you wanna go to lunch with us?" I asked, seeing her leg propped up on three pillows. "Oh my... girl, what the hell happened to your leg?"

"Ohh umm... I fell. I was trying to work out, I started jogging, and I stepped into a pothole. I twisted my damn ankle and popped my knee out of place."

"Damn boo. Well, sorry for you. I will make sure Destiny bring you a doggy bag back. We about to go to The Cheesecake Factory and I'm treating. You have fun here though, we about to bounce."

Getting up from her bed, I headed back out the room. Destiny was standing at the door waiting impatiently; especially since she heard me say I was treating her greedy ass.

"Let's go, boo." We got in my car and headed to the restaurant.

"Sooo, what's new?"

"Besides the fact that you're about to be an auntie."

"Shut the hell up! You are not pregnant."

"According to the four tests that I took, I'm very pregnant."

"Yaaaay, I'm going to be an auntie. It was about time one of y'all got pregnant. I was starting to have baby fever, but now I can just brush that feeling off. You know Desire' has been fucking with Knight's little brother."

"Ugh, that weird mother fucker. It's just something about him that creeps me out."

"Girl, yes. She's been with his ass a lot lately."

"I guess. I wish them the best with that. It's good she finally let Domano's ass go though. He was a whole mess too. Oh, oh, oh, I almost forgot. The other night Knight was out of town on business, and he told me he was almost home. I forgot to unlock the door and I didn't remember cause my ass was playing in this pussy something good you hear me?" I joked. I can laugh now since it's over with but at the time the shit wasn't funny.

"Tell me why some strange mother fucker walked in my shit and raped me with a fucking dildo?"

"I know you fucking lying, bitch!" she exclaimed. "How did he get in if you didn't unlock the door?"

"That's the part I couldn't figure out. I only thought it was Knight because he knows where my spare key is so I never even thought about it being someone else. When that damn hand covered my mouth I swear it scared the shit out of me. I tried so hard to fight him off, but nothing would make him move until he heard Knight's voice. Then the little fucker jumped out the window. I was so fucked up, for real. That was the scariest day of my life, sis."

"I'm sorry you had to go through that but wait, why would a dude fuck you with a dildo? That's some weirdo shit right there."

"Tell me about it. The police wasn't any help at all. It's like I try to get over one thing and boom I'm hit with another issue. I don't get it," I said, shrugging my shoulders.

This shit is starting to seem so unfair. First my sister, then I get attacked twice. I'm almost scared to have this damn baby because ain't no telling what the fuck gone happen next for me.

We pulled up to the restaurant and got out. It was packed, but I was willing to wait because I was starving like Marvin, whoever the hell that is.

"Isn't that your ex, Alex?" Destiny nudged me to look up from my phone. I locked eyes with him and the beautiful woman that was on his arm. He wasted no time moving on to another woman to fuck while his damn wife is at home dying. He can't lie like this is his cousin because this bitch looks nothing like the one he had at the Aquarium.

"Yep, I'm about to go speak too."

"Girl! You are crazy... but hold on, I'm coming with you." Destiny grabbed her purse and hurried next to me.

"Hey Alex," I spoke.

"Hey...hey Summer. How have you been? I haven't seen you in years," he said loudly. My face turned up with confusion.

"What are you talking about, I just saw you las—"

"Let me introduce you to my wife, Dawn," he blurted out, cutting me off.

She turned to me with the biggest smile on her face. Her skin was golden brown, and her teeth look like she been to three dentists to get work done to make them so perfect. She was slim with the biggest rock sitting on her finger. The bitch doesn't look like she got cancer at all.

"Hey, it's nice to meet you." She reached out for my hand.

"It's nice to meet you as well. It's good to see you are doing well. It was just last week Alex told me you were dying from lung cancer." She pulled her hand back quick as hell. He had me all the way fucked up if he thought he was just gone lie to me to get some pussy.

"Nooo, that's not what I said. I said she was flying from Kansas."

"Boy, no you did not."

"I thought you said you hadn't seen her in years, so how were you able to tell her I was flying in from Kansas?" his wife asked with her arms folded.

"Girl, he told me a lot while he was deep up in these gu..." Destiny pulled me away before I could finish my sentence.

"Fuck him, our table is ready, and you have a whole little family now to worry about. Let him live with them lies he told on his wife."

Agreeing with her, we took a seat at the table and ordered our food. I was still a little pissed that he lied to me, but it's cool. That's why his ass still rocking the ooowee knot on his head that Knight gave him, lying ass nigga.

KNIGHT

"Where do you see yourself in five years?" I asked Summer as we sat on the couch.

She was laying between my legs watching some crazy movie on Netflix. She decided instead of us going out to dinner tonight that she would cook and play this game called Talk. I ain't never heard of that, and I honestly think she just made that shit up. I don't know what type of game Talk is, but I hope the winner gets pussy in the end.

If not, I'ma have to order one of those big human dolls to fuck cause I ain't going to long without getting inside that warm pussy of hers. All I ask is that for my two grand that it comes with a ton of lubricants, or I'm gone be one dry, dick stroking mother fucker.

"Umm, fortunately, my plans have been altered a tad bit. I had plans to move out of the state once I graduated from CSU. The plan was to find me a nice little state to settle down in and to find me a nice good paying teaching job. Also, I plan on going back to get my Masters. A baby wasn't in my plans until I was married, but it seems like God had another plan for me."

"Moving away is still an option. It's not like I want to stay here for the rest of my life. I wouldn't want you to put your dreams on hold because of the baby. Once you finish school, who knows where we might end up."

She started smiling hard as hell. I would drop everything here in a heartbeat and move wherever she wanted to go. I can always hire someone else to run my centers in the city and open up new ones where ever we move.

"Where do you see yourself with me in the next hour?" she asked.

"I thought we were talking long term?" I questioned.

"I know, I know, but my pussy just started thumping, so apparently, she's horny as hell."

"In that case, in the next hour, I see myself deep inside of you. Listening to you scream out, *Oh god*, over and over again as I sucked your soul out that sweet spot of yours."

"Hmm, yes papi! Let's get this shit started now." She jumped off the couch and headed straight to the shower.

She always thinks her ass is in the movies and be wanting me to eat her pussy in the shower while water is running all over us. She just don't know that I be two gulps away from drowning. It's hard as hell trying to eat her pussy and swallow all that water that's dripping off her at the same damn time.

When she got inside the shower, she started wetting her hair, and I watched as it went from straight to curly. Once I stepped in, she surprised me and went down on her knees slowly. Taking my dick in her mouth, she started sucking my shit like it was a Popsicle on a hot summer's day.

My toes were popping so hard in the water that it sounded like somebody was eating some Hot Kruchy Curls.

"Damn, girl," I uttered.

Grabbing her head, I started fucking her mouth. That shit was feeling so good that I had to get control of the situation before I came to soon. I was stroking her mouth long and deep, making sure she had no choice but to deep throat my shit. Moving faster and faster, I could hear her mumbling and moaning because she was so into the shit.

"What the fuck?"

Feeling something warm covering my dick, I opened my eyes and saw throw up all over my shit. She jumped out the shower and went right to the toilet to finish. I was mad as hell cause that shit was nasty as fuck. I was just about to nut too. Washing the throw up off my dick, I got out the shower and got on my knees behind her as I moved her hair back so she wouldn't throw up on it.

The way she was throwing up she had the perfect arch in her back and my dick got hard again. She kept throwing up, and I slipped my dick back in to get this nut.

"I know you playing, right?" She asked with her face deep in the toilet. Shit, it's either now or never, she'll be ok.

❧ 18 ❧

MARQUISE

One week later

Since I made Tameka leave my crib, my ass has been at the strip club every chance I got. I would spend my time with MJ during the day, and when I leave the house to handle business at night, I call Destiny.

Summer has been having so much going on and wanted to be alone, so she couldn't watch him but suggested I let Destiny do it. Surprisingly, she didn't even hesitate to come over late at night. Some nights it almost sounded like she was waiting on my call. MJ has become so attached to her that he would cry to go home with her. At first, I was skeptical, but he begged me to let him go with her.

She even spent a few nights over here before and it took a lot for me not to try something. She would walk around with those little ass sleeping shorts on, begging me to bend that ass over.

I can't even front like I haven't been checking her chocolate ass out every time she come around. They been around my sisters since we were kids and I've always looked at them like little sisters too.

Unlike her hoe ass sister Des, Destiny is actually a good girl. MJ told me she be asking questions about me, like if I'm still seeing Meka or if I talk to anyone else.

That shit be making a nigga smile for real. I'm always open for love, but since I'm single I have been a little hoe.

His mother fucked me up with her drug addict ass and Meka just wasn't motherly enough for me. I just may have to give Destiny a shot though one day. Take her to dinner and thank her for helping with MJ. Then if everything goes well I might give her this dick she been begging for.

She and MJ are out for pizza now while I sit back at the crib and watch ESPN.

Hearing the bell ring, I headed down the stairs to see who it was.

"What the hell?" I said, swinging the door open. "Why are you at my damn door?" I asked MJ's mom. She was standing here looking like the lady on Tyler Perry's *Diary of A Mad Black Woman* movie before she burst into the church singing.

"I wanna see my son, Quise. I miss him so much." She tried to force a tear out, but I wasn't falling for that shit. Pulling my phone out, I Face Timed Destiny's phone and asked her to put MJ on.

"Here." She rolled her eyes, but I didn't give a fuck.

"Hey, mama's boy."

"I'm not a mama's boy. I'm daddy's big boy."

"I miss you, MJ." FaceTime ended flashed across the screen. I reached for my phone back as soon as I saw that shit.

"I guess he was done. You can go now."

"Marquise, I'm really trying to get better."

"Next time say that shit without the white residue on your nose. Get the fuck off my doorstep!" Slamming the door in her face, I headed back upstairs.

She like doing those fly by night walk by's and think everybody's world is supposed to stop. MJ is tired of the empty promises and shit, so I am. Before she started doing all of this shit she was so fucking beautiful. Her body was banging, her pussy was spectacular, and her head was the greatest. Shorty was the girl every nigga wanted, but only one nigga had, and that was me.

When she got on that shit, she started shriveling up like a dick in cold water. I can almost bet that pussy is loose as a goose now too. You know crackheads will do anything for a piece of crack. I had no respect for her as a woman and most importantly a mother.

Flopping back down on the couch, I grabbed my remote and started flipping the channels. *Unsolved Mysteries* was on, and for some reason, that man voice always creeped me out. I turned from that shit fast as hell. So many crazy things have been going on with my family that we should have our ass on there.

Thinking about the things Summer was saying to Knight at the hospital, I decided to call him up to talk to him again. Since the last time we spoke I didn't go into much because he was too excited about the baby.

But, something wasn't right, and if he is in the middle of this shit, we gone have a serious fucking problem.

"Aye, meet me at the club," I spoke through the receiver to Knight.

I sent Destiny a text letting her know that I was about to step out for a minute and to take MJ home with her. Once I'm done with this, I will just swing by to pick him up. Grabbing my keys off the counter, I headed out the door. Jumping in my car, I headed downtown to get to the bottom of this shit.

Sitting at the light, I looked to my left, and I couldn't do shit but chuckle and shake my head. MJ's mom was on the side of an abandoned building, giving the best neck her dry mouth ass could probably muster up. I started to blow her head off, but the light turned green. I already knew she was on bullshit, and that's why I never feed into that shit.

About 30 minutes went by, and I was finally making it downtown. Traffic was crazy on the E-way, so I took the streets. Pulling up in front of B-live, I parked and headed right to the office. A few girls were out giving dances, but it wasn't thick in here yet. Taking a seat, a few minutes later Knight walked in.

"Fuck wrong with you, bruh?" I asked noticing the frustration on his face.

"Summer's ass got a nigga running around here with blue balls. Talking about she don't want to have sex again until after see the doctor. That's three week away, I can't take this shit."

"Damn that's fucked up. I won't keep you long, but this shit has really been bothering me. Everything with what happened to her the other night. Tell me what you know so far? Cause I'm lost in all of this."

"She told me about your sister and the person wearing the hoodie. My brother actually owns that clothing line. The other night when she went out for Desire' birthday, she was attacked in the alley by someone wearing the same thing."

"She never told me about that."

"After that shit happened I had my brother look out for her while I was gone with Skillz. I told him her information and everything."

My wheels started turning in my head when he said that, but I didn't say anything to him. I was gone make a visit to see this mother fucker myself.

"Interesting."

"He wouldn't have a reason to do this shit, so I'm not blaming him at all."

"Well, somebody got something against my sister, so I gotta figure this shit out."

We chopped it up for a little while longer, and both went in different directions. I headed right to TK's house to see what this little bitch had to say about all of this.

DESIRE'

I waited outside of the doctor's office on my sister to come back and pick me up. This week has been so fucked up, and I hate I can't get around how I want to. I was running last week and twisted my fucking ankle. So much for trying to stay in shape, right?

I've been hoping around this bitch looking crazy. Seeing the car pull up, I stood up the best way I could with these raggedy ass crutches. Noticing MJ was in the car with her now caused me to shake my head. She is so head over heels for Marquise ass, and she doesn't even know it yet.

"Take me to TK's house," I said with an attitude.

"When you started talking to Minnie Mouse this strong?"

"When they beat the hell out of Domano. TK has always been my fall back guy, and this time was no different. He was there willing and waiting to be my knight in shining armor."

"A whole lil dick mess. His ass should have picked you up then instead of me wasting my damn gas." I chuckled.

I gave her ass five dollars to take me to and from the doctor. She better be lucky I didn't ask for my change. Ever since she started hanging out with Marquise, she acts like she doesn't have time for me anymore. It's either she has to work, or she's watching MJ lil uglass.

That whole damn family is starting to make my pussy itch worse than the time Domano ass gave me crabs.

"Whatever." I stared. She shrugged her shoulders and kept driving. I sent him a text to let him know I was on the way there.

Getting out the car, I headed up the flight of stairs as quickly as I could. I needed this pussy licked, and maybe this time he will keep his finger-dick in his pants so that I won't be confused between the two.

"Daddddddy, I'm home!" I called out.

"What's good, ma? How is that leg doing?"

"It's cool for the most part. I will be ok in a week or so. I do need some special attention though. I'm sure that mouth of yours will take this pain out in no time."

"Nah ma, not today. You can suck this big dick though."

"HA!" I laughed out loud before I knew it. "My bad, my bad. You can't be serious, right G? Your dick won't even sit on the tip of my tongue. Your dick ain't no bigger than Dros' dick from *She Wanted the Streetz, He wanted her Heart* by A.J. Davidson."

"Who?"

"Never mind, anyway meet me in the back and bring some ice." Grabbing my crutches, I limped my way to the back of the apartment.

Hearing him getting the ice out the refrigerator brought a smile to my face. He knows his dick is too little to get sucked. I laughed again to myself as I started undressing. Lying in bed with my leg propped up on a few pillows, I waited for him to come in.

"Ouch... What the fuck?" I yelled right when another piece of ice hit me in the head. "TK, what the hell is wrong with you?"

"What the hell is wrong with your rioting pussy ass calling my dick little? You know how many times I fucked your sour pussy ass and had to fight back the smells of every STD, Domano gave yo ass!" he spat, and I was shocked as fuck. Before I could speak, another piece of ice hit my ass on the lip.

"Bitch!" I yelled, trying my best to get out of the bed to get to his shriveled dick ass. "You got me all the way fuck up."

"Nah, ya pussy is the one that's fucked up. Get the fuck out of my damn bed." Limping over to him quickly I got close enough to swing on him, but the gun he pulled on my ass made me rethink my life.

"Look, Desire'. We got so much shit going on right now, and the first thing you did was come in here talking about getting your pussy ate."

"I don't have shit going on. I did my part, and now you just have to do yours."

"Exactly what is your part?" Our necks snapped around to the bedroom door, and there stood Knight and Marquise.

Fuck my life. I thought to myself as I tried to cover my body up.

"Ain't nobody checking for that Chlamydia-filled ass pussy," Marquise hissed.

"Why in the hell is everyone talking about my pussy? Shit!"

"You got bigger problems than that, baby girl," Knight stated.

"DESIREEE', I came back to give you this ugly ass coat you left in my car! Where are you?" I heard Destiny yell out, and moments later, she stepped into the bedroom holding my coat.

"What are y'all doing in here?" she questioned.

"Let me see that?" Marquise asked, reaching for the coat. "I'll see you at the house in a little while we have some business to handle here."

"Umm Des' you straight?"

"Yea sis, I'm ok. Go ahead."

After making sure Destiny was gone, he turned back to TK. "Somebody better start talking," he stated, cocking his guns back and pointing them at me and TK.

19

KNIGHT

The more I sat at home and thought about this shit the more and more things started pointing to my brother, but why? When Marquise called me over, and I told him about everything that happened, I could instantly see he was thinking the same thing.

To stop him from killing my brother, I told his ass it wasn't him because he had no reason to do all of this. I wanted to talk to him first, but when I pulled up to TK's crib, Marquise pulled up right behind me. Since I had a key, I let us in, and it looked like we walked in right on time.

"Somebody better start talking," Marquise blurted out once he saw the black hoodie with the tiger face on it. I thought it was weird that Desire' had the coat now, but come to think of it, the other day TK said he let his girl take it home with her.

"TK, SPEAK!" I yelled out.

"Look all of this shit was her plan," he confessed.

"Nah you a lie, you started this shit." They started going back and forth pointing fingers at each other like look ass kids.

"You know what, I ain't scared of neither one of you bitches. If you ask me that lil crazy bitch got exactly what she deserved."

BAM!

"Don't call my girl a bitch!" I spat, hitting my brother in the face. "She ain't do shit to neither one of you simple mother fuckers."

"Nigga, fuck both of them. I didn't know it was two of them mother fuckers until Summer walked into your office that day."

"You know what, I knew something wasn't right the other day when Summer had mentioned you saying I told you about her twin sister. I never mention she was a twin. All I said was her sister was killed. Then you pop up at the restaurant right when I told you where she was and that she was good so you didn't have to check on her. You showed up on some sneaky shit anyway."

"Y'all talking too much bullshit. Let's get down to the real shit," Marquise stated as he walked up on TK. "Did you kill my sister?"

"With no hesitation!" he replied, staring down the barrel of Marquise's gun. "She killed my brother and thought she was going to get away with him since she was crazy as a Betsy bug. I was there the night they got into it. I was drunk off my ass, so I passed out in the back room and woke up when I heard the commotion. She was having one of her little crazy spells again where she thought mother fuckers were after her.

"Turk, get away from the window now." Sunny whispered.

"What? Why?"

"They're out there watching me. Just waiting on me to step outside so they can kill me. I won't let them get to me. I'll kill them mother fuckers first...all of them. All 2,345,678 of them. They are all out there standing by the window. Watching... waiting... lurking... and staying.

"Girl, calm yo three flights of crazy ass down." Turk blurted out and started laughing.

"Nope, I told you I was going to kill them and I'm going to do just that."

"With What Sunny? What you gone talk them to death like you doing me right now?

"With this."

"I told you to stop playing with my guns Sunny. Gimme my shit and go lay yo ass down until I drop you off at home." All of a sudden I heard loud noises sounding like someone was stomping really hard on the floor. By this time I got

out of bed and peaked out the room. Pissed because them mother fuckers wouldn't let me sleep.

"YOU'RE TRYING TO SET ME UP! I TOLD YOU I'M NOT GOING OUT THERE. YOU'RE ONE OF THEM!"

"Don't aim that thing at me girl."

"AAAAAAHH." She screamed out then, POW POW POW POW POW POW.

He was just trying to get her to calm down, and she unloaded the clip on his ass. When she saw the blood coming out of his head, she snapped out of that crazy and ran out of the house.

I came from out the back and called the police. I told them that I found him like this and never mentioned her name mostly because I didn't know if Sunny was her real name or not. I wanted to get her ass back my damn self. It took a year to find her, but I did.

Thanks to her big brother for giving her that bomb ass job at the strip club. After I fucked the shit out of her in the alley, I cut her fucking throat. I refused to let that bitch take another breath while my brother was buried because of her."

Marquise was just standing there like he was waiting for the right moment to blow his head off and truth be told I didn't know what to think. I didn't know if I wanted to thank TK or beat his ass for what he did.

He already knew Turk had a problem with beating bitches, and it was either she killed him, or he was most definitely going to kill her for pointing the gun at him. Turk didn't play games like that at all.

"FINISH!" Marquise's voice boomed throughout the room. "What happened to Summer since you are in the mood to spill your guts before I kill yo ass?" TK started laughing, and that shit pissed me off.

"Now Summer was Desire's plan. She never could stand Sunny for fucking Domano, so she always wanted to get revenge on her, but I beat her to that part. Summer was next on her list because she felt like Summer knew the entire time that her sister's crazy ass was fucking Domano and all of a sudden decided to tell her."

WHAP!

"Call my sister crazy one more fucking time and yo ass ain't got to tell me shit else. I'm just gone kill you and funky pussy at the same fucking time."

"Man, y'all on some more shit. You're my brother but standing over there with a gun pointed at me too because of a bitch. She killed your brother, and you don't give two fucks about that part, huh. Summer's pussy must be made of gold for you to overlook that part.

POW!

"KEEP TALKING!" I spat, after shooting him in the shoulder.

"FUCK!" he hissed. "I killed Sunny, and Desire' put me up to come after Summer while she was at the club."

"You a lie!" she yelled out. TK's neck turned to her so fucking fast.

"BITCH, IS YOU SERIOUS! How about y'all ask her ass what really happened to her leg. She damn near broke that mother fucker jumping out Summer's window that night." *Now that's some nasty shit for real,* I thought to myself. "You told me what club you were going to for your birthday but some kind of way yo ass didn't show up. She was right in front of me drunk as hell, so when she went outside, I followed her, and if it weren't for some dumb ass stopping me, I would have finished her ass that night.

I wanted to kill her mostly because I didn't know which one it was that killed my bother. I thought the shit was over with when I got rid of the first bitch. After a while I forgot the name she went by and all I remembered was that face, but when another bitch with the same face walked in your office, I was confused.

So, they both had to go. Desire' came over one day and told me she wanted me to help her get rid of someone. She knew about the girl I killed over my brother, but she never knew it was Sunny until I told her that the girl I killed had a twin and that I ran into her at my brothers place.

I guess she put two and two together. When that shit added up to four, she wanted in. It was all her plan to do them both the same way so that it could look like a copycat murder. It was just my luck you walk yo love sick ass into my office and tell me to look after your girl while you were gone.

That was like music to my ears, bruh. Desire' left out with my coat and said she had a plan, and I would come in after her and handle the rest. That whole nasty ass dildo was her idea. The shit was real comical to me though. Who the fuck rapes a bitch with a strap on dildo?"

He laughed, and as soon as his mouth opened up wide, Marquise sent three shots through his head, I didn't even flinch.

I just turned my attention to Desire' and pointed my gun.

"Your turn."

SUMMER

"You good, baby girl?" my daddy questioned, pulling me out of the daydream I was in.

I was sitting at the table having lunch with them and my sister-brother Markell. Knight left me to go to a meeting. So when mama said she cooked burgers and fries, I got my ass up and came right over here. Every time I'm left alone, all types of thoughts flow through my head. I be begging his ass to come right back home when he leaves the house.

Honestly, I'll just be glad when I can move away from all of these memories, and maybe my life can go back to normal. I want to get my sister out of my head and stop trying to play detective. I told Desire' give me a week, and if I didn't find out anything then I would be done, so I'm done.

As far as my situation, I don't know where to begin with that. I don't know if it was a male or female, so I gotta put that shit behind me too.

"Yea daddy, I'm ok. I'm just thinking about graduation and my plans afterwards."

"You're finding a job here, right?" he asked, but it was almost like he was telling me at the same time.

"No daddy, nothing has changed from the first time we talked about what I wanted to do once I graduated. I'm still going to move away from here. This city has brought me so much heartache that I refuse to spend anything past a day here after I graduate."

"I don't want to lose you too."

"But daddy, you're not losing me. I'm still going to be only a phone call away. It may be a flight to visit, but still only a call away. You know I hate leaving you two, but I have to do this for me," I assured him.

My daddy has and will always look at Sunny and me as his little girls. There's no growing up in his eyes. My mother, on the other hand, she understands, and she's going to make my father understand too because regardless of how much he pleads, I'm still leaving.

Hearing my phone ring in the other room, I got up to answer it.

"Hey baby, you back at home?" I asked Knight.

"Nah not yet, I need you to meet me somewhere. I've got a surprise for you."

"Oh gosh, what is it?"

"You mean who is it?"

"Huh! What are you talking about, Knight?" I was starting to get worried, and you could hear it all in my voice.

"I'm about to text you an address, meet me there now." My heart started racing because I could hear the seriousness in his tone and it was really freaking me out.

I went back into the living room and told my parents I had to go. My mama wrapped up my food for me to take with me. I hugged them all before I left out the house to meet Knight. By the time I made it to the car, a text was coming through with the address. I unwrapped my food and ate it on the drive up to Schaumburg.

⚙

Pulling up to one of Knight's old centers, I noticed Marquise's car was the only one here. Confused, I got out to see what the hell was going on. Right when I walked in, Knight and Marquise met me at the door. Looking around the room, I was trying to figure out what I'm here for.

I thought they had some gifts or some shit for me, and I know damn well he's not about to give me this old ass building that his ass didn't even want anymore.

"Come here, sis. I got something to show you," Marquise requested. He grabbed my hand and walked me over to the darkest area in the room.

"WHAT THE FUCK DID Y'ALL DO TO HER?" I screamed out. These fools had Desire' tied up with dildos stuck in every part of her body that has a hole. I rushed over to get her untied and gagged.

"You might wanna leave her like that once we tell you what's going on," my brother spoke up. He was now standing in a corner smoking a blunt while Knight stood there with a gun pointed at Desire',

"Y'all better start talking and tell me what the hell is going on."

"I thought you should know that your little bestie is the one who raped you the other day. Your little bestie is also the bitch who had you set up to get attacked in the alley after the club."

My mouth dropped open, and I was standing there in complete shock. How could she do something like this?

"But wait, there's more," Knight said.

"We also found out who killed Sunny," Marquise intervened.

"WHAT? WHO DID? DID SHE DO THAT TOO?"

Before they even replied, I ran up to her and started beating her ass. I was hurt, broken, confused, and completely fucked up in the head. This was my girl. Even though she was a sneaky bitch, I had no idea she would do something like this.

Feeling my body being lifted off her, I was placed in a chair by Marquise.

"She didn't kill her, TK did, but she did find out that he did and instead of her being a good bestie and telling you what happened, she decides to plot against you and try to set you up next. Now, my question for you is, what are you going to do about it?" Marquise asked.

Looking up at Knight with tears in my eyes, I couldn't help the thoughts that were flowing through my head. "Did you know?"

"I had no idea he did that shit. I promise Marquise and I just found out at the same time. I would have been hurt his little ass for doing that shit if I had known."

"He's telling the truth, sis. He didn't know but again, what are you going to do about it? She can go meet her boyfriend TK in hell, or you can torture her ass until you decide to just blow her fucking head off. Either way, the bitch has gotta die."

I didn't know what I wanted to do but I felt like death would be entirely too easy for her.

Walking up to her, I had tears in my eyes but this bitch was like a sister to me. Yea we might pump heads, fuse and fight but all sisters do that shit.

"Just tell me why? I've always been a good friend to you. Never once would I have done something so dirty to you. Why Des? Why?"

"Bitch fuck you! Once my memory came back I remember seeing yo face once you knocked my ass out. Then gone act like yo ass didn't know what the fuck happened. You always wanted to be the perfect one. Summer got the good grades, Summer had it all. Summer even got my man."

"Hol' up! You ain't have a chance in hell to get me even if I wasn't with her. You been a hoe since you started yo period. Fuck out of here with that shit." Knight blurted out.

"Yea whatever. Anyway I don't have time for this shit. Y'all got the info y'all need so let me the fuck go."

Looking at her, I couldn't do shit but shake my head. "Give me a minute."

Getting out of the chair, I stepped outside and made a quick phone call. Heading back inside, I took the gun from Knight and walked over to Desire'. She looked at me with fear in her eyes not knowing what I had planned to do to her ass next.

We went over what I wanted her to say over and over again until she had that shit right. Every time she fucked up, I would make one of them hit her ass in the face.

BAM! BAM! BAM!

POLICE, OPEN UP!

The detective from the hospital came in with three more cops behind her.

"Good evening, Summer. I'm glad you reached out to me. So, you have something for me?" I pointed over at Des.

"She has something to tell you." Tears started pouring down her face, and her lips were trembling.

"I-I killed Sunny Daze, and I was the one who raped Summer. You will also find a body at 17874 Eastern Avenue in Bellwood. It's the body of Tristian "TK" Knight. I killed him and his brother, Turk Knight."

With no hesitation, they started untying her and putting handcuffs on her. She said everything exactly how we rehearsed it. It was life in prison, or Marquise was going to blow her fucking head off.

"You have the right to remain silent. Anything you say can and will be used against you in a court of law." The police read her rights to her as they walked her out of the building.

"Thank you, Summer. I'm sorry I couldn't be the one to bring justice to you, and you had to find all of this out on your own. Either way, I'm glad this is settled, and you can now breathe easy. I wish you the best, and we will be in touch." I nodded my head to her and watched her walk out of the door.

"You good, shorty? Knight questioned.

I had to think about the answer before I replied. I can finally say, yes, I am good without lying. This has been one helluva ride for the past few months, and things are finally slowing down for me. My life has been a whirlwind, but now I can finally live my life and be free of worrying, crying, and watching my back, thinking someone is out to hurt me.

Life can't get any better than this.

❧ 20 ❧

SUMMER

*O*ne *Week Later Graduation*
        "Summer Daze."
        Walking up to receive my degree after four long years at Chicago State University, this has to be the happiest day of my life. At one point I thought I wouldn't make it. I thought after the first year things were supposed to get easy, it didn't. I pushed and pressed through all of the things I went through and still came out on top. My sister was the main reason I kept going. After she was killed, I definitely wanted to give up. That was until Marquise made me see how far I've come, and how Sunny wouldn't want me to give up.

She was my personal cheerleader, my best friend, and literally my other half. So, this degree is not just for me, but for her too. She enrolled for the spring classes, but unfortunately, her life was taken from her before she had a chance to start.

"CONGRATULATIONS!" my family yelled in unison.

"YOU GO, GIRL! WALK THAT WALK, SIS!" Markell yelled out, making my mama and daddy side eye his ass.

I had to laugh because he almost let the dick out of the bag on their asses. All of my family was standing there cheering with flowers and balloons with *Congratulations* on them. My eyes fell on Knight, and he was looking so damn sexy. He wore this gray Armani suit that I picked out for him, and it made his chocolate smooth skin stand out even more. Everything about this man is sexy, and I can't wait to spend the rest of my life with him.

KNIGHT

Watching my shorty walk across that stage made me the happiest baby daddy ever. I wasn't here in the beginning when she had to go through a lot to finish school, but I was here in the end. I made sure she didn't have to worry about a thing once she finished.

Not only that, she wanted to move away, and I made that happen too. She has been talking about moving to Charleston, South Carolina, so I flew out one weekend and found us the perfect house. It's right down the street from three great schools. As smart as she is, either one of those school would be lucky to have her teach there. She walked over to me with the biggest smile on her face, and I made sure I mirrored the same thing.

Man, I love the shit out of this girl. Even though both of our families took a piece of us away from us, we're still gone fight through this shit. I promise to love her till our dying day and be the best father to our kid that I could ever be. This Dark Knight once had a dirty past, but Summer Daze brightened my life up with her love, and I wouldn't change any of this for the world.

DESTINY

After hearing everything that Desire' did to Summer, I was hurt and pissed off. Summer and Sunny have been our girls since forever, and this is shit you just don't do to best friends. I was grateful to Summer for not killing her ass. She told me that she didn't want me to experience the hurt that she has felt since losing her sister.

We cried and laughed together, but most of all, we got over everything and promised to have each other's back through all of this. Marquise and I have been seeing a lot of each other. He is a little over the top, but nothing that I can't handle. I fell in love with MJ, and even if Marquise and I don't work out, that's gone be my little guy regardless.

MARQUISE

I know I came off as a fucked-up person when it came down to Tameka. If you asked me, she deserved that shit, and I wouldn't change shit about what I did. I bet she gone learn now not to give a child those hot ass chips or she gone end up with another hot ass, literally. After getting everything handled with Desire', they gave her ass 60 years to life for all of the bodies she had under her belt. If I were smart, I would have pinned a few more on her ass too.

That bitch deserves every year she got, and TK deserved getting his fucking head blown off. I may act like I don't have a care in the world unless it's pertaining to MJ, but just know for my sisters, I'll move mountains. If Knight isn't careful and he feels like he wanna get on some slick shit, I'll have some hot lead waiting for his ass too. Anyways, y'all be easy though, I'm about to go to the store to get me some Takis.

Deuces

THE END

THANK YOU

THANK YOU FOR READING, AND IF YOU HAVE JUST A LITTLE MORE TIME, PLEASE LEAVE A REVIEW.
   -A.J.
   Keep Reading For a Sneak Peek!

SNEAK PEEK

DOPE BOYS NEED LOVE TOO - COMING MARCH 12th
GHOUL

She didn't want to go out and suggested she cook dinner for me. I loved that shit. My last bitch did nothing like this. Cooking to her was warming up something she got from her mama house. That shit was good but still she ain't cook the shit herself.

Pulling into my garage, I got out and went inside.

Ima fuck you like I'm tryna pay bills.

Georgia Power, Cable bill, Babysitter, tonight you will... ooohh!

Let me take out my weave don't wanna mess it up while I'm deep up in them sheets.

A lot of time spent on my knees, but I damn sholl ain't praying.

Removing my gun from the small of my back. I started walking around the house to see where the music was coming from. This is the first time I was pissed that my house is big as fuck. Making my way upstairs, I followed the music into my bedroom. Dropping my gun, I couldn't do shit but shake my head at Kyanne freak ass laid across my bed. Her hand was so far in her pussy, all I saw was the Tiffany bracelet I bought her for her birthday dangling from her wrist.

"What the fuck you doing in my shit Ky?"

"Don't you miss me daddy? I came all the way over here to surprise you with some of this good pussy."

"Nah and you need to get out my shit for real. Ain't you fucking with Ace now? Shouldn't you be over there giving him that sink-hole ass pussy or cleaning his pockets out how you used to do my shit?"

"Don't worry about him. I'll take care of him later but right now, it's all about you baby." I was kicking my own ass right now for not changing the code to my gate. The bitch must have parked her car down the street cus I didn't see her car in the drive way.

BUZZ BUZZ

Hearing that sound made my heart stop. Air was at the gate and this bitch was laying in my bed looking like she was giving her ovaries a fist bump.

I started tying all of my sheets together cus I had to get this bitch out of here. Dropping it out of the window, making sure it was long enough to get her ass half way down. She can drop the rest of the way. The bitch got big feet, I'm pretty sure them big bitches will break her fall.

"You got me all the way fucked up. I know you don't expect me to jump out the window. Ima leave out this bitch the same way I snuck in, through the laundry shoot."

"Bitch, I don't care how the fuck you get out but yo ass ain't going through my front door." Grabbing her by her hand, I pulled her to the window.

"Listen, if you do a spread eagle as soon as you feel the breeze, the wind from the west may fly you towards the pool. That's the safest place to land. From there I need yo ass to haul ass cus the Rottweiler gone chase yo ass until you are off my property."

BUZZ BUZZ

Once the buzzer went off again, I wasted no time pushing her ass out the window. She either gone grab the sheets or use her feet, either way she is getting out my damn room. I watched her until she landed in the pool before I turned away to let Air inside the gates. Kyanne has a long run from the back of the house so by the time she makes it to the front, Air will be inside.

Opening the front door, I gave Air a once over and my dick started to brick up. she was standing there with the same look on her face that she had the first night I saw her at the restaurant. She was rocking this tight ass Adidas fit with some matching shell toes. She was dressed down, but she had my dick up like a motherfucker.

"Why you got me waiting like this? I started to turn my ass around and take my dinner to my brother."

"I'm sorry, I had to get rid of a pest." Right when I said that, all I heard were my dogs barking and Kyanne hauling ass out the gates full speed. Pulling Air inside before she turned around to see why they were barking. I took the bags out of her hand and lead her to the kitchen.

Noticing the bags were hot and smelling good, I looked at her ass sideways.

"I thought you said you were cooking dinner."

"Nah, I said I was getting dinner. I wasn't about to let the steam from cooking all this food mess my silk press up. This shit took too much time to get done." Shaking my head at her. I couldn't even be mad cus she was looking to damn good.

"I got steak, shrimp and loaded potatoes, is that ok?"

"I'm allergic to shrimp shorty."

"Me too, that's why I put them on the side just in case. Toss them out, it's cool."

"I'll take them to my dogs, they need a treat for the work they just did. Gimme a minute." They were running back up to the house when I stepped outside, I placed the food on the porch for them and went back inside. Air was in the kitchen putting everything on plates. She was moving around my kitchen like she owned the place. I just sat back as she sashayed around the room. It was like her ass was moving to the beat of its own music and my dick was ready to beat on her drums.

"Gotta any A-1?" She asked pulling me out of my trance. Getting up, I walked over to the cabinet she was standing in front of. Pressing my dick up against her ass as I reached above her head to get the sauce down.

"Ghoul, don't play with me like that. You could have asked me to move instead of putting that little ass door stopper against my ass."

"Ha! Girl I'll fuck yo world up with this
big boy. Don't ever play me like that."

"Yea aight."

"Keep talking shit, ima bend ya ass over the dishwasher."

"Hush and come eat."

"That's all I needed to hear. You ain't never gotta tell me that shit twice." Putting her on the counter top, I ripped her pants off. She was so in shocked she didn't even stop me. Moving her panties to the side, I pressed my lips against her pussy and just took in the smell. She smelled like a meadow of sweet smelling roses. Letting my tongue take over, I started feasting and I wasn't stopping until her nut was covering my chin.

Sucking her pussy and fingering her at the same time had her ass howling. She had a good grip on my dreads and I knew then she was about to cum.

"Fuuuuuck!!!" she moaned, and I stayed right there making sure I sucked her dry. Leaning up, I looked at her and watched as her chest rose up and down from
breathing so hard. I walked over to the table and sat down so we could eat.

"You gone come eat or sit there like I just snatched ya soul."

"Shut up. Let me go clean up first. Where's the bathroom?" she grabbed her purse and I lead her down the hall. I came back with her some basketball shorts to put on. I had no intentions on doing that, but she was looking so damn good, I just had to taste it. Trust, it was well worth it too. Even her cum tasted sweet and I most definitely can't wait to get inside her.

She came out the bathroom and I couldn't do shit but smile. She even made my basketball shorts look good.

"You owe me a pair of pants." She stated, taking a seat at the table.

"I'll give you the world shorty. All I need is the chance to make you mine. There is no limit to the things I will do to put a smile on your face, to make you cum like that, or to make you fall in love with me." Not saying a word, she just started blushing and cutting into her steak.

COMING MARCH 12!

BOOKS BY A.J

The Street King I Feel For: A Misunderstood Love Affair 1-2

Cherished By A Boss 1-3

She Wanted The Streetz, He Wanted Her Heart 1-2

Creeping With The Enemy: A Savage Stole My Heart -Collaboration With Latoya Nicole 1-2

I Saw Mommy Kissing A Savage- Standalone

KEEP UP WITH A.J

Facebook: Ashley AJ Davidson
Instagram: AJ_penpusha
Email: Ajdavidson@outlook.com
Like Page: Author A.J Davidson
Author Amazon Page: amazon.com/author/ajdavidson86

CPSIA information can be obtained
at www.ICGtesting.com
Printed in the USA
LVOW13s2114100418
572944LV00014B/1674/P

9 781986 384469